A New Beginning

God's Second Chances

Barbara Eubanks

A New Beginning

God's Second Chances

Editor Lori Boatfield

Barbara Eubanks

Whosoever Press books may be ordered through booksellers or by contacting:

Whosoever Press
10749 AL Hwy 168
Boaz, AL. 35957

www.whosoeverpress.com
1-256-706-3315

ISBN: 978-0-9987724-6-2
Library of Congress Control Number: Applied For

Printed in the United States of America

Whosoever Press Date: 11/1/2017

Table of Contents

Roman Road to Salvation

Foreword

My family has been a part of Alabama medicine for 119 years. I guess I was born to follow this profession. I am of the belief that you MUST thank GOD for what you have, not what you don't have. We are blessed in this country to have freedoms not available to most of our world. Challenges that we face build our character, and we must realize that failure is not an option for those who wish to grow in our faith and integrity.

I was paralyzed from the neck down in 1965 by Guillian-Barre syndrome and wore braces (like Forrest Gump) until I shed them in first grade to play football. When I was a junior in high school, I was awarded the first of two All State awards in football at Westminster Christian School in Gadsden, Alabama. I was blessed to have the size and athletic ability to excel in sports. I played competitive golf from age 8 until current time. A hunting accident at age 44 cost me my left arm above the elbow. I am a firm believer that disability is a state of mind to which I will not succumb. I have won eight national amputee golf championships by maximizing my gifts, not my shortcomings. Life is too short to surrender seconds, minutes, or hours basking in self-pity. Since my accident I have continued to practice surgery with the help of my partners and nurses and believe that surgery is a mental discipline that requires knowledge and experience and courage.

All people are challenged in their walk with events and encounters that stress their faith in God and humanity. We must understand that although we are merely sand on the earth each grain has purpose and importance. Maximizing our impact on relationships is our duty to be able to sleep at night. Each individual has an intrinsic strength that yearns to be expressed. I will always believe that our Creator means for us to work daily for His glory, regardless of our weaknesses.

Lucian Newman, III, M.D.

General Surgeon

Preface

Bermuda's bright sunlight awoke the middle-aged honeymooners. The day began as gloriously as had the previous thirteen. Thad and Molly had not only enjoyed all the sights Bermuda had to offer, but the pleasure they found in each other was unequaled. This truly was the beginning of the rest of their lives – lives made richer by their uniting.

Later that morning on the plane, with her head leaned back, eyes closed, and a satisfied smile on her face, Molly silently reflected on how great life was at that moment. Her new marriage was a unique mixture of great excitement and a comfortable peace. She held Thad's hand, and he occasionally squeezed hers just as a simple expression of his love. Thad was the antithesis of Jack. How could she keep from comparing him to the man she had given her youth to, the man who had fathered her children? Her many years of trying to be a perfect wife for him, the perfect pastor's wife, were rewarded by his belittling her, making her feel insufficient in every way, regardless of how hard she had tried, and then by his crushing her and throwing away his family by having an adulterous affair. Only through hindsight could she see how totally selfish and self-consumed he was – only by being married to Dr. Thad Simmons, who was completely the reverse. Never in her wildest dreams could she imagine a kinder, more loving and attentive man as Thad.

Their honeymoon had been filled with adventure, laughter, and romance – not the young passionate kind, but rather a coming together in a warm, loving, unrushed way that rightly puts the other's pleasure before one's own. Never had she been as totally satisfied as she was now in body and soul. Never before had Molly ridden a jet ski. Never before had she experienced the exhilaration of riding high in a parachute being pulled by a boat. Never before had she felt as totally relaxed as she did by lying under the warmth of the sun on a beautiful beach with a man who entirely adored her and didn't fail to tell her so.

Her reverie was suddenly interrupted. This was not ordinary turbulence; the plane's vibration and the irregular sounds of the right engine signaled trouble. She involuntarily clutched Thad's hand, and he gripped hers in response. *Surely God hasn't brought us this far only to let it end in our beginning.*

"Mom sounded so happy when I talked with her on the phone last night. Her unfettered delight echoed in everything she had to say. Benji, wouldn't it be a nice surprise to arrange a welcome home celebration for mom and Thad? A group of us – close family and a few friends – could meet them at the airport. It would be unexpected and would be just to show them we share in their happiness."

"You always have the smartest ideas, Sis. I wish I had thought of that and could take credit for it. Let's do it. You just tell me what to do or who to call and I will be at your beck and call, as usual," Benji laughed. "Then if it goes well, I'll just tell Mom it was my idea all along." Caitlin gave her brother a playful nudge in his belly in retaliation.

If anyone ever deserved a new lease on life, it was Molly. She had remained faithful and supportive to Jack Pate even after he fell into a web of sin that destroyed his ministry and led to his downward spiral. Even after he left her for another woman, even after the accident which took his second wife's life and left him a broken invalid, Molly extended Christ-like love for him. She took him back into her home, not as a husband, but as one of God's children who needed her nursing skills. This took a mighty toll on her as she sacrificed sleep and health to care for him; that scenario had almost cost her Thad.

In the beginning of their marriage, Jack had been more considerate. For a time he appreciated Molly as a helpmate. As he became more and more successful in the ministry, he morphed into an egotistical, self-absorbed man, a man who felt he deserved illicit sexual satisfaction and excitement when it came in the form of Darcy, a young woman with a sordid past. In spite of his actions and hurtful treatment of her, Molly had set the example in forgiveness for the family, the church, and through it all, she even developed friendships with unlikely people. Before he died, Jack repented and mended relationships. Caitlin no longer hated her dad, as she once did, nor did her brother Benji.

It wasn't unexpected for Bob and Caitlin, with Emily in tow, and Benji to be a part of the welcoming committee, but the remainder of the small gathering – Sawyer Thomas, Gloria Downs, and Celeste Downs – might seem strange to those who didn't know their history with the family. Well, not too unusual for Sawyer to be there, but for his fiancée, the woman who bore a child – Celeste – conceived in a college tryst with Jack, was puzzling, especially to those who didn't know Molly's kind, accepting spirit.

After Celeste became suspicious of the mystery surrounding her mother's account of her father's "death," she set out on a quest to find him or, at least, his family. And she had. Through many conversations and visits, Molly realized Celeste had no fault in her untimely conception, and she had received her into the family graciously, as had Benji and Caitlin. After all, the three shared in the same father's DNA. Even after a visit where Gloria had told the sordid details of hers and Jack's college affair, her pregnancy, Jack's placing the blame on her and denying his paternity, the family embraced her also.

It was truly a God thing when she met Sawyer. They brought out the good in each other and forgave each other their pasts. Sawyer became Molly's confidant after Jack's failings. Molly was strategic in bringing Sawyer back into church and helping him resolve his own anger toward his faulty preacher-father and toward God.

In the baggage claim area of Atlanta's Hartsfield airport, Caitlin just couldn't stand still. She hopped up and down trying to get the first peek of Molly and Thad as she anticipated their coming down the escalator. "I can't wait to see their reaction when they see us all here. I know they must be on the ground by now. It is 3:45 and their ETA was 3:20."

"Ah, settle down, Sis. You are acting more childish than your daughter." Little Emily was totally entranced as she watched the empty baggage carousels make their rounds. "You know how airline schedules are these days. It would be a small miracle if they had landed on time."

"Benji," said Sawyer, "stay here with the girls and hold on to all these welcome home balloons; Gloria and I will find an info board to see if their flight has landed yet. With the way the wind is howling out there, I would guess they are in a holding pattern or have been diverted. They're probably not allowing any planes to land in this stormy weather."

Soon, the couple returned with disappointing news. Sawyer reported that all incoming planes had been rerouted due to a tornado warning in the area. "The agent strongly suggested we go home before the warning reached the airport vicinity. He gave me the web site where we can follow the progression of their flight."

From the intercom, the flight attendant attempted to calm fears. "We are experiencing trouble with an engine, but be assured this plane can operate safely with the one remaining. Stay calm and remain seated with your seat belt tightened securely." Margo, the seasoned attendant wanted to add, *and pray.* She had made this flight many times, as well as hundreds of others, and knew trouble when she heard it. She had not needed her last message from Captain Brent Jacobs, the pilot, to know they were in immediate danger. Capt. Jacobs had also warned her they were flying into a thunderstorm, and Atlanta was under a tornado watch. Jacobs knew they had passed the midway point between Bermuda and Atlanta almost an hour before, so returning to Bermuda was not an option. He knew he had to find the nearest place to set the crippled bird down. His message to Atlanta's air control was short of a Mayday, but it definitely had an air of urgency. "It seems I ran into a flock of birds which has stalled my right engine and may have slightly damaged the other one. I need clearance to land at the nearest inland airstrip."

The answer was not what Jacobs wanted and only added to his consternation. "Atlanta and surrounding airports won't be options due to high winds and a possible tornado forecast. We are diverting flights to South Carolina. If you can get there before the storm does, you can land at KMYR." Myrtle Beach had a suitable airport, but Jacobs knew his airspeed had been hampered by losing one engine and having the other crippled. He doubted he would make it that far.

Margo and Chip, the second flight attendant, went about the plane insuring seat belts were tightened and that electronics and carry-ons were stowed away safely. Chip spotted a three-year-old playing with a metal truck. Talking to the mom, Chip said, "Ma'am, would you put away the toy?"

"Now why should I do that? It is keeping my son pacified, and if I take it, he will pitch a fit."

Not taking the time to gently cajole, Chip, understanding the urgency of the situation, substituted his normal people-pleasing personality, with grave sternness. "Ma'am just put it away – NOW. Otherwise it may become an airborne projectile before we are on the ground." Fear replaced her stubbornness, and she obeyed and stowed the toy.

Some of the other 150 passengers on the small plane were already panicked. A young mother, flying with a toddler and an infant, stopped Margo. "Will you notify my husband that we aren't landing in Atlanta? He's there waiting for us. How will I get to where he is?" On every hand, Margo and Chip tried to assuage passengers' concerns while trying to conceal their own.

Acknowledgments

So many family members and friends have contributed to this novel. They have let me "bend their ear" as I asked for their expertise in their particular area. For their willingness to share information and personal experiences, to each of them, I say a big Thank You:

To my son Dr. Steve Eubanks, Jr., you are always my go-to-guy when I need any input about medical matters; your willingness to help out your mom is such a blessing.

To my dear friend and pilot, Don Spurlin, your input about airstrips suitable for the crash landing near the area in question brought a realistic touch to the crisis. Thanks much.

My brother-in-law, Col. Grover Randolph Southerland, who flew innumerable missions over the Ho Chi Minh Trail during the Viet Nam War, I thank you for your technical input about problems a plane might encounter. And as always, thank you for your heroic service to our country and for faithfully loving and caring for my sister Sylvia as she battled cancer.

To my sweet one-armed surgeon, Dr. Lucian Newman III, who considers me another mother, my gratitude goes to you for giving me some insight to the spiritual, emotional, and physical journey of an amputee. You just might recognize your quotes coming out the mouth of my character Dr. Newell. I would lie if I said I didn't have you in mind when I fashioned him as an outgoing, positive surgeon. Much of the rest of his saga is strictly fiction and is not intended to characterize your marriage or life.

To Corey Garmon, my former student and hero who lost both legs and suffered other significant injuries while fighting in Afghanistan, you were so patient and generous in recounting your entire traumatic story with me which gave me much fodder for my making Benji's tragic injuries more genuine. A million thanks.

To Dr. Glen Sexton, another amputee, thanks for sharing your ups and downs with prosthesis adjustment. I thank you for your contribution and to the bravery and determination in achieving something many thought impossible – adjusting to two artificial legs when you are past seventy.

To Kim Duckett - the CP (Certified Prosthetist) who offered freely his technical expertise about the fitting and adjusting to prosthesis, your information was invaluable. Finding you was like finding a jewel because your information came from a person who knows personally some of the joys and the challenges. Joyce, the prosthetist character in the novel, shares some of your story.

To my faithful Sand Mountain Lit Chicks – Gay Martin, Lori Boatfield, Alice Duckett, and Shirley Mitchell - thanks for listening to my readings from my drafts each meeting and offering honest, but encouraging, input.

Jenny Sims, my dear friend, thank you for always encouraging me to get on with it and finish the novel and for reading and reacting to the draft.

For my faithful readers of my first novel, thank you for inspiring me to write this sequel – Beginnings.

Introduction

If you have read **A Web too Tight**, you have met the Pate family and their friends and are privy to the joys and heartaches they have experienced. But life is not stagnant; it keeps moving on, just as do the lives of these fictional characters.

Beginnings picks up where **A Web too Tight** ended. It isn't necessary to have read the first novel to get caught up in the drama surrounding these characters. Enough background information is given for the story to stand alone.

Because of sagas of plane disasters, amputation, medical problems, and other calamities in this novel, I had to rely on quite a few people to get details as accurate and realistic as possible. These contributors are listed in the acknowledgements, along with their areas of expertise. Not the least of these is Dr. Lucian Newman, III, my one-armed surgeon, who graciously wrote the Foreword and offered great collaboration.

When one chapter of life ends, there is always a new beginning. So it is with the Pates. I trust you will live vicariously through the life-situations of the characters in Beginnings, crying at heartbreaks and smiling through victories.

1

A Rough Spot

Never had Thad and Molly experienced such turbulence. Molly, being typical Molly, showed more concern for those around her than for herself. Across the aisle sat a college student from Bermuda who was making her first trip to the U.S. to accept a swimming scholarship from Auburn University. She made little noise but the tears raining down her face and her vise-like grip on the armrest signaled her great fear.

"Sweetie, would you like to hold my hand? Sometimes it helps just to hold on to someone. That and prayer help me. Why don't I pray for all of us," suggested Molly. "What is your name?"

In a voice that quivered like Jell-O, the girl answered, "Maliki." Maliki gladly took the hand Molly offered.

In a soft voice, Molly began, "Father, we are in a really rough spot right now. It appears our plane may make a less than safe landing, but we put our trust in you. Hold Maliki tightly in your arms so she will feel safe and secure. Please help the couple in front of us with the small child." One by one, she prayed for those around her, and for the flight crew, and finally, she prayed, "God, I

2

know you haven't brought Thad and me this far unless you have a greater plan for our lives. Please hold us in the palm of your hand. But regardless, my faith is in you. May your will be done."

Her prayer had not gone unnoticed by all the people around her. 'Amens' echoed throughout the cabin.

Another message from the captain interrupted the reverence of the moment. "Ladies and gentlemen, this is Captain Jacobs. I am going to be brutally honest with you because we are in this metal cocoon together. I don't believe we can make it to Myrtle Beach through this storm on one crippled engine. Therefore, I am about to attempt a landing on a strip nearby that is not designed for a plane of this size, but it will beat nothing. Therefore, I'm asking you – no, telling you – to take every precaution per the flight attendants' instruction to brace for a rough landing, a very rough landing. We probably will run off the end of the strip, but I'm doing everything in my power to keep us as safe as possible. Now, call on a power mightier than mine."

Minutes later the plane swayed to the right and then back to the left. Jacobs tried with all his might to straighten the bird and make things as smooth as possible, but even with all his might, he failed in his attempt. As

3

they touched down, or better said – slammed down, on the small runway earth-shattering sounds of metal scraping roared over the screams. Sparks lit up the plane like a spot light. The impact forced the plane from one wing to the other, back and forth until pieces of the wings lined the path behind them.

The captain didn't lie. The landing was a teeth-shattering, plane-breaking one. Although passengers were buckled in and items were stored as instructed, pieces of metal sailed through the cabin as parts of the plane broke up on impact. Screams echoed throughout the plane, some from fright, but others from injuries. Many had bleeding gashes from flying objects, while others had greater damage. One flight attendant, with the help of a muscular volunteer, was able to get the inflatable slide activated, and she professionally instructed passengers to make their way, if possible, to that exit to deplane.

"Molly, let's move to the exit." After a lack of an immediate response from her, Thad gave her a soft shake and repeated, "Molly, Molly." He noticed she had not escaped airborne debris herself. A streak of blood on her forehead revealed she had also been struck by something.

In a delayed response she said "Oh, yes, we need to make our way to the exit and see if we can help."

Moving Into The Triage Mode

As they got to the exit, Thad identified himself as a doctor to Margo, the shaken but uninjured flight attendant, and Molly as an R.N. Margo found comfort in this handsome, professional doctor's demeanor who would know more about handling these passengers than she would. "Do you have an emergency kit and supplies, such as bandages and antiseptics, nearby?" asked Thad. "We can begin seeing to the injured."

"Oh, thank you, thank you," the attendant replied. "We store kits near all exits." She quickly reached overhead, unstrapped the box and passed it to him.

As soon as they were down the slide, Thad's first order of business was to clean and bandage the minor laceration on Molly's forehead. "I'll take a closer look at that later." He made a mental note to also check her out for a possible concussion.

After finding a grassy, smooth area a safe distance from the plane, the injured who were able started making their way to the make-shift emergency area. Thad and Molly, with their years of medical training, knew that the loudest cries weren't true indicators of the severity of injuries. As a matter of fact, they both knew that silence often signaled greater problems. The two started to turn chaos into calm with their composed presence with word and treatment. Moving into her R.N. mode, Molly began the triage, lining up patients according to how urgently they needed attention. Some of the uninjured passengers brought those non-ambulatory ones to Molly's area. Going down the row of patients, Molly quickly assessed the situation and had the unconscious ones moved to the head of the line. One of those was Maliki. Molly knelt beside her and saw she had not only a severe bleeding laceration on her head, but she also had a badly mangled leg. Molly feared it was so crushed that it would have to be amputated. Her pulse was thready and her breathing weak. After doing what she could on the spot, Molly labeled her an immediate priority. Molly remembered Maliki had said she was going to Auburn University on a swimming scholarship. Molly mused about how this would change the girl's life and dreams forever. There was no time for lengthy prayers, but Molly said silently, "Lord, I've done what I could for this sweet girl. Please take her in your protection and hold her tightly in your comforting arms." Molly didn't stop with prayers just for her; she breathed a prayer for each of the injured in turn.

After she and Thad had treated several of the most severely wounded, Chip, one of the flight attendants, made his way to Thad. "Doctor, could you possibly come with me back to the plane? I'm afraid Captain Jacobs took the brunt of the blow. We can't get him off the plane. He is unconscious and his foot is lodged. I think he has other injuries too, and we don't want to move him without your guidance."

"Are you okay taking over here?" he asked Molly.

"Sure, but take care of yourself." Then in hushed tones said, "You know there is some smoke coming out of the engine."

An impeccably dressed businessman came near as he saw the insurmountable task that lay before Molly.

"I have no medical knowledge or experience, but I will help you if you instruct me in what to do," he offered.

Molly said, "There are parents with screaming babies and young children. I believe their injuries to be fairly minor, but they are scared. Could you go and help with them?"

"How? What should I do? I'm not a very good parent for my own children."

"Maybe pick them up and speak softly, reassuring them they will be okay. And, sir, breathe a prayer for these who are more critical."

"I can do the first part, but I don't know how to pray. I've never been too much into that religious stuff. Although I think I did say, 'Help me, Jesus,' as we were coming down." He already regretted offering help. He knew he wasn't cut out for this task in anyway.

Molly continued her work, being very efficient, but replied to the man, "If you said that, you do know how to pray."

Thad looked around to assess what help might be available. He saw the muscular guy who had helped inflate the slide. He quickly commandeered him to assist, as well as a few other able-bodied guys. "I need you to help me get the captain down, if we can." By that time the plane was empty except for the captain, but it was dark with acrid smoke. Thad began by identifying himself and trying to rouse the injured Jacobs to no avail. The gurgling sound in the man's chest did not bode well. Thad did what he could to brace Jacob's head with a makeshift board. "If we can manage to pull back the metal that has his foot trapped, we need to get him and ourselves off this smoking time bomb."

The strong guys moved into action, prying the metal open with an iron bar they located in a nearby closet. When they extricated Jacob's mangled foot, Thad splinted it with an umbrella one of the guys found and handed him.

As though he was no heavier than a child, the young men lifted him and took him to the exit. The biggest of the three sat in the edge of the exit and instructed the others to place Jacobs in a sitting position in his lap. "I can brace him this way." He yelled to another buddy outside the plane to be at the bottom to soften the landing. Without hesitation, the others slid down and helped move Jacobs to the safe area. Thad was the last one down. Just as he neared the emergency area, a series of explosions began behind him and the plane became a blazing inferno. "Thank you, God," he spoke aloud. The sentiment was echoed by many.

By this time, emergency vehicles had made their way to the site. After a few minutes, Thad and Molly had stabilized Jacobs as well as they could and instructed the EMTs to take him first. His signs of an internal bleed put him as priority one, even ahead of Malika. Visual injuries could wait, but gauze and band aids were useless with an internal bleed. Only surgery could stop that. In a short time, Thad and Molly were relieved of their duties and ground crews and EMTs took over. Even though Molly was ready to relinquish her duties, she couldn't put Malika out of her thoughts.

"If I can find a phone, I need to let the children know why we aren't in Atlanta." A man, who was grateful for Molly's first aid attention to his head wound, took his phone out of its holder on his belt and handed it to her. "Letting you use my phone is mighty poor pay for your first aid."

There was a great bond of camaraderie among the victims of the crash – an unspoken sense of gratefulness for having survived.

A Witness

After the emergency personnel took over, those shaken, but without serious injuries, were taken to a safe area by airline officials and debriefed. They were assured they would soon receive flight information for their final destinations and would be flown there as soon as possible. Molly turned to Thad and said, "If it's all the same to you, I had rather rent a car and drive home." Thad held Molly by her narrow shoulders, looked deep into her blue eyes and asked, "How do you do that?"

"What?"

"Read my mind," Thad replied with his endearing one-sided smile. "I was just about to suggest that, and by the way, you are a rock. Nobody could have organized that chaos and so perfectly triaged. I wish I had married you a hundred years ago." Molly laughed at the absurdity of his last comment, but reveled in his adoration.

"Hmm. I couldn't help but overhear your part of your conversation," injected a nearby passenger. Molly recognized him as the man who had come to her aid and offered willing, but awkward help. "My name is Ralph Cochran. I sat a few rows behind you and have observed your kindnesses to passengers before and after the crash. I called and ordered a limousine; it's here, waiting for me, and it would be my honor if you would allow me to take you to Atlanta and on to wherever you had planned to go from there."

"Oh, that is not at all necessary," Thad answered. "We will just rent a car and be on our way."

"Handling that stress-ridden situation back there has to have taken its toll on you two, both physically and emotionally. The least I can do is to let you rest as we go home. But I really have a two-fold purpose in this. I not only want to take you home, but I also want to ask you some questions as we travel. I couldn't help but notice your supernatural calm and your prayers. I am a successful executive with IBM, but I realize wealth and power can't provide the peace you two have exhibited. I want you to explain how I can have it."

Thad and Molly turned to each other, knowing what the other's answer would be. They believed in divine appointments and recognized this as one. Although they had made it off the plane with very few personal belongings, they gathered what they had salvaged and entered the limousine.

Cochran began by telling them more about himself. "I am married to Selina, a model, and have three troubled teenaged children – Thomas, sixteen; Dahlia, fourteen; and Jackson, thirteen. We have anything we want that money can buy. I don't mean that as bragging, I'm just giving you the facts of our distressed existence. Although we live in the Buckhead area in a generous estate, there is no happiness there. I would say in our home, but it really is not a home in the warm sense. Ours is a household of turmoil; we are constant hurling insults at one another. Selina resents me for my impregnating her times three and causing her a great struggle and near starvation to maintain her model figure. She is involved in an adulterous affair, and not her first. I can't be too critical of her, because I've had my share of other women as I travel about two-hundred days a year. Our children stay in trouble at school for disrespect, and Thomas has already had several brushes with the law for drug use. I'll have to admit I haven't played much of a role in the rearing of our children. Mostly, I've been an absentee father, even on the few days a year I've been home. I didn't know how to parent children and had even less interest in doing so. Today, as we had our brush with death, I realized I would trade everything I own for the complete serenity you two displayed. Would you tell me how I can have it? As I earlier told Molly, I know nothing about prayer and, until now, have had no interest in anything religious"

Cochran had opened the door for a witness, and Molly and Thad walked through. Thad explained that their joy was rooted in their faith in Jesus Christ. "You can have it too, if you repent of your sins and, in faith, believe and accept Christ as Lord and Savior of your life." Ralph had his driver find a place to pull off the road so he could look at the couple with complete attention.

Molly, who had been trained in various evangelistic programs, chose the Roman Road to Salvation* to share; the scriptures that had been in her mind for years quickly and naturally rolled off her tongue. She began explaining how he could have the same peace and hope in Jesus that she and Thad had. She used the scriptures about how he could obtain this and presented explanations of each. She told him so clearly and personally that anyone, even a child, could understand, especially an intelligent seeker like Cochran.

John 3:16 says -
"For God so loved the world, that He gave
His only begotten Son, that
whoever believes in Him shall not perish,
but have eternal life."

14

Romans 3:23
"for all have sinned and fall short of the
glory of God,"

Romans 6:23
"For the wages of sin is death, but the free
gift of God is eternal life in
Christ Jesus our Lord."

Romans 10:9-10
"that if you confess with your mouth Jesus
as Lord, and believe in your heart
that God raised Him from the dead, you will
be saved; for with the heart a
person believes, resulting in righteousness,
and with the mouth he
confesses, resulting in salvation."

Romans 10:13
"for Whoever will call on the name of the
Lord will be saved."

Thad then interjected, "Ralph, what Molly
has told you may seem too simple for such a
major step in your life, but if you accept and
do these things in faith, salvation can be
yours. Would you like for me to lead you in
a prayer of salvation?"

Cochran had no hesitation in bowing
his head and repeating after Thad a simple
prayer of confession, repentance, and

acknowledgment of Christ as his Lord and Savior. Tears streamed down his face as he told Thad and Molly, "Thank you, thank you, thank you. You have just given me life."

"No," said Thad, "Jesus gave you that new life a long time ago; you just accepted his gift today."

"I understand," conceded Cochran. "Could I ask one more favor? Would you come and share this with my family soon? I'm not sure I can remember all you explained to me, and I want to get it right when I share with them."

"Anytime," the couple replied in unison. "I'm sure you would do great; all you have to do is relate to them what Christ has done for you and how you accepted his free gift of salvation, but we would love to meet them and be your back-up." They squeezed each other's hand. "I think whatever we went through today was well worth it if it meant gaining a new brother in Christ," voiced Thad.

Home Again

Home had never looked so good to Thad and Molly. When they arrived, they immediately knew a homecoming celebration awaited them when they saw all the cars in the driveway. "Won't you come in with us and meet our family," invited Molly.

"I want to do that at some later time, but you need this private reunion, and I want to go home and share what has happened in my life with my family. I don't know how they will receive the news that I have accepted Christ and am a new creature. I don't know how they will take this initially, but maybe I can show them that I'm a changed man."

Thad assured him they would pray for him. He also told Cochran about a new believer's bible that would be helpful. He handed this new Christian a business card because Cochran had asked for contact information.

"Are you two okay?" "Were you scared when you knew the plane was going down? How many were injured?" – The entire group waiting for the honeymooners all threw questions at them at once. Thad would try answering one, only to be assaulted with five more questions. Finally Benji interrupted and reasoned, "You think we oughta let them in the door and put their suitcases down before we interrogate them?" Laughter erupted and then Sawyer took the bags from Molly and Thad and placed them in the bedroom.

"I'm so glad you are here and safe. We were all just so worried about you. You don't even know yet the danger you escaped if you had made it to Atlanta. A tornado wiped out the C terminal at the airport. We just barely got back home when it happened," interjected Gloria.

"We want to hear all about your crash, but first, come on in, eat some of the good food piled high on the table, and we will get the details after you relax some. I've had to keep Benji beat off it until you got here." Caitlin hugged her mom once again and then gave Thad a bear hug. "Sometimes it takes near tragedy for us to know just how much we love you and how important you are to us." She flicked a tear off her cheek. Thad and Molly grabbed her and returned the love.

As the group sat around the table, Molly said, "Before we get into all the accident elements, we've got to tell you about the good that has come from it." She and Thad related to them the story of Ralph Cochran's conversion. "I've always told you children, good could come from bad situations.

A Promise Becomes A Reality

Soon Molly and Thad resumed normal activities – church, entertaining, gardening, volunteer projects, mission trips, vacations, and Molly's favorite – time with family.

Normalcy had begun to replace the trauma and the drama. Thad was in his recliner, absorbed with his latest mystery, while Molly sat by him in her favorite chair reading her "Home Life." Thad turned to her, pulled off his reading glasses and said, "Molly, do you think we will ever hear from Ralph Cochran again? His coming into our lives at such a difficult time still amazes me."

She pulled her feet off the ottoman and gave her full attention to his question. "Thad, I don't know." She wrinkled her forehead as she did when she was deep in thought. "I just have to believe that's not the end of our relationship with him because he was so visibly and genuinely changed."

Just as Molly entered the house from her vegetable garden one sunny morning, the phone was ringing.

"Mrs. Simmons, you may not remember me. My name is Ralph Cochran. We met after our emergency landing a few months ago, and you and your husband gave me the greatest gift anyone could ever receive. You introduced me to Jesus."

"Oh, I remember you well, Mr. Cochran," which was a miracle within itself because, there were some events missing in her memory these days.

"Please, call me Ralph."

"Only if you will drop the "Mrs." and call me Molly. You won't believe that Thad and I were just talking about our encounter with you just a few days ago."

"The reason I'm calling is there have been changes in our family since we met that only someone like you could believe. We have so much to share and so much to ask. Could we take you to dinner Saturday night?"

"No," replied Molly bluntly. Then she continued more kindly, "I want you to come to our house for a country dinner. I have just brought in an abundance of fresh vegetables from my garden and am itching to cook all of them. Besides, our living room would be more conducive to conversation than a restaurant would. Be here at 6:30 and dinner will be on the table." Cochran knew there was no arguing that point because of Molly's confident authoritative air.

"Will your children be with you? We would love to meet them."

"Not this trip. We will have to tell you about the changes in their lives too. They have some prior commitments this weekend. We do want them to meet you later."

Saturday arrived, and when Ralph and Selina entered the Simmons's home, no sweeter aroma had ever filled their nostrils. The table was loaded with creamed corn, green beans, fried eggplant, okra, tomatoes, green onions, cornbread, fried chicken, and other southern delights. With sweet tea to drink and homemade ice cream for dessert, the Cochrans felt they had reached Utopia. Not only was the food inviting, but the Simmons were the warmest hosts imaginable.

Thad said, "Ralph we could never forget you and the impact you had on us. Your accepting Christ that day reassured us that good could come from a bad situation."

Selina began, "I've wanted so to meet you two ever since that eventful day. It has been a day that initiated a new beginning for all our family. You can't understand what a different Ralph came home to us. He could take my wildest insults about his new-found faith without batting an eye or lashing back. After his transformation, I knew I wanted to change too. Pride, fear of change, reluctance to give up the life I knew had prevented me from telling Ralph this or even letting him have any idea of this feelings for months. Finally, miserable with our rich, but empty lifestyle, I knew I would gladly give up everything to have what he did. I finally asked him to tell me how I could have this peace too. He shared with me the beautiful gift of salvation."

"That's one thing I want to ask you," injected Ralph. "Would you go over the scriptures and the plan of salvation you shared with me? I just want to make sure I didn't leave out anything important when I told Selina. I'm confident God has made a change in her life, but I'm insecure in my knowledge about holy things; I just want to make sure I got it right."

Thad smiled and said, "Ralph, we will be glad to go over what we told you, but there is no doubt that God used whatever you told Selina to bring about this wonderful change."

Leaving the house with full stomachs and peaceful hearts, Selina and Ralph hugged Molly and Thad like they were lifetime friends and thanked them profusely for their influence.

"No, argument about it, the next dinner is on us," commented Ralph. As the couple drove home, Selina told Ralph, "I made another decision tonight. I have decided to give up my modeling career and dedicate my time to being a better wife and mother."

"You don't have to do that, Selina."

"Yes, I do. A model's life is a self-absorbed one. I rarely think of anyone's needs but my own – my diet, my beauty, my wants and desires. I think I got a holy tap from the Lord tonight reminding me of this. I just wish I could be like Molly someday."

"God made us all and gave each of us different abilities, but it sure wouldn't hurt if you could learn to cook like her." They both enjoyed a laugh at that.

Not So Good News

"Ma'am, I've been noticing you for a while now. Can I help you some way?"

"I'm sorry to have to admit it, but I can't find my car."

"What are you driving? I'll look for it while you rest."

Molly had walked the grocery store parking lot for over an hour because she didn't want to ask for help. She knew she was in big trouble because she couldn't even remember what kind of car she had. She phoned Thad and had to tell him what was happening.

"Sweetie, you drove the red Mercedes convertible. Don't you remember?" Thad was really concerned.

In the days following, Molly experienced several other disturbing incidents. "Thad, have you seen my reading glasses? I've looked high and low for them and can't find them in any of the places I usually lay them."

Thad smiled, reached up and pulled them from the top of her head and handed them to her. "Mystery solved."

"You are the sweetest husband a girl could have. You don't even make fun of me when I do ridiculous things." Molly tiptoed and gave him a peck on the cheek. Thad gave her a loving squeeze. "I must confess, I did one better than that the other day when I called you from the grocery store. I don't know if you remember my pausing for a minute. I suddenly thought I had left my cell phone in the store. I asked the buggy boy to go see if it had been turned in. He sweetly said, 'Ma'am, I believe you're talking on it.' I know he must have thought I had totally lost my mind." They both laughed, but Thad's chuckle lacked sincerity.

A few nights afterwards, Molly sat in her easy-chair reading and Thad had been out by the pool sweeping the deck and was coming in the back just as the doorbell broke Molly's concentration. "Well, what a nice surprise." Caitlin and Bob looked at each other astonished. "Mom, you called yesterday and invited us to come for dinner. Don't you remember?"

Trying to cover for her lapse, she answered, "I don't know why I said that. Sure I knew you were coming. We just decided to take you out for dinner tonight."

Molly didn't fool anyone, especially Thad, who had noticed earlier she had seemed to forget the kids were coming for supper. He had not questioned her about it, because she had been distraught over recent forgetfulness episodes. He knew they could take the kids out to eat but also knew Molly

26

normally would have spent the day cooking for them.

She turned around and saw Thad had come in. "Caitlin, Bob, and Emily have just arrived. Why don't we take them down to The Broken Spur for dinner? I'll go get dressed if you will come in and entertain them while I get ready."

Thad welcomed the opportunity to discuss Molly's condition with Caitlin. After hugs and greetings and Molly's departure to the bedroom, Thad said, "I'm afraid Molly is showing some early signs of Alzheimer's. She has had several disturbing occurrences of memory lapses lately. I've even noticed she doesn't take the attention to her appearance she always has. Just as you saw her, she looks disheveled most of the time. I want you two to be observers while you are here to see if you notice a difference in her."

Caitlin readily agreed. "Thad, I've been noticing a change since about a week after your return. I just wanted to blame it on her adjusting to retirement, the trauma of the crash, and to a new married life, but I can't deny that I've been concerned. What can we do to delay the symptoms or help her recover from this?"

"To be truthful, there isn't a great deal that we can do. There are a few medications that are often prescribed, but I've never known of them making much difference, but let's not jump to conclusions too soon. We will need to confer with Benji and your half-sister, Celeste." Celeste had been included in all family decisions, celebrations, and conferences ever since they had discovered her, or rather since she discovered them. "With their approval and support, I plan to get Molly a thorough neurological work up. It may not be easy, because Molly is too smart not to know there's a problem, but she is very much in denial. Normally, Alzheimer patients don't know they have it, but with Molly's medical experience and her strong sense of just knowing, she is the exception. In cases like this, people often want to delay putting a tag with the ailment. It is as though it doesn't exist as long as we don't call it by name."

"Well, why rush confirming our suspicions then, if there is no viable treatment?" Tears overflowed Caitlin's eyes. "She doesn't deserve this. She has been through so much, has been so faithful, and for once is enjoying the true happiness she deserves. Why would God allow such a thing to happen to her?"

Bob embraced his wife and said, " Caitlin, don't you remember the many times she has told us that bad things do happen to good people, but that God can work good through them and receive glory? This is a time we must draw on the strong faith she has instilled in all of us."

"Maybe so, but I'm not ready to give up the mother I've always known."

"Caitlin, I'm not ready for this either. Molly and I have so looked forward to a life together. I'm pretty strong, but I just don't know if I'm emotionally equipped for dealing with a wife with Alzheimer's," added Thad. "If it is what we suspect, I promise you I will stand by her and do my very best to care for her, but I feel so inadequate to do anything about this horrid disease."

Molly emerged from the bedroom smiling. "Now that I'm all cleaned up, I think I should start dinner."

The group looked at each other. Thad fixed the situation without reminding Molly of their plan. "Sweetie, let's just go down to The Broken Spur and you won't have to cook tonight." With that, the decision was made – both to go out for dinner and also to get Molly tested.

Praying For A Miracle

Only three months prior, returning from their honeymoon, Thad's salt and pepper tousled curls against his newly-tanned skin enhanced his debonair image. Today, those same qualities, along with his furrowed brow, simply made him look years older. Alzheimer's disease certainly wasn't his specialty, but he had seen it in patients enough to clearly recognize its symptoms and to dread the future; Molly had exhibited so many of them that he was expecting the tests to confirm his strong suspicions. He found his role as a family member to the patient, rather than the doctor, most miserable. He sat in a small waiting room with head in hands. He had called in professional favors from colleagues at Georgia Baptist in Atlanta, one being a world-renowned neurosurgeon, and had been able to schedule Molly for a complete neurological workup the next day. The private room was tense as each family member handled his or her fear in different ways. Benji was antsy, moving from one chair to another, from the restroom to the water fountain, and then to the vending machines, really not hungry for anything. Tears had rolled down Caitlin's cheeks off and on all morning as if she already knew her mom would never be the same.

The fog of tension and fear finally became so heavy in the room Celeste felt something had to be said or done to bring some calm. She began, "I may be the wrong one to suggest this, but I've just been thinking how different this scenario would be if one of us had a problem and Molly was out here in our place. I know what she would do – she would take the lead and tell the group to 'lean not on our own understanding,' but to pray and trust God. I know all of us have sent up prayers all morning, but do you think we could hold hands and pray aloud? Maybe if we hear each other call upon God in this time, we will find the strength to accept the worst if that's the way it turns out, but have faith that God will work some miracle and heal her mind."

"I knew we got you into this family for more than adding beauty to our gene pool, Celeste." Benji continued, "That is exactly what Mom would have suggested if it was one of us going through all these tests." This brought the entire group out of their individual musings and to their feet.

"I'd like to begin if that's okay," began Thad with voice trembling. After pausing to regain his composure, he ran his fingers through his already tousled hair, and finally prayed. "Dear Lord, I know you are great and know all things. I acknowledge just how weak I am in comparison. I ask that you take my stumbling words and make them the prayer they should be in this time. I am pleading for a miracle for Molly just now. Whatever her problem is, I ask you to heal her. I know none of us is worthy of your abundant grace and mercy, but Molly comes as close as anyone on this earth can. She has always stood as a stalwart tower of faith and service. Please make her whole just now." With that, Thad broke down and wept like a child, which was totally uncharacteristic of him.

Benji reached out and put his arm around his stepfather. "God, grant us peace and acceptance of your will, whatever it is in this situation, but I beg you for a healing miracle for my sweet mom."

One by one, the gathering humbled and became more acquiescent to God's will, but also strengthened in their faith that God was in control of the situation and trusted Him for a miracle for Molly. As they wiped their eyes and started toward their seats, they saw Dr. Slaughter, the one coordinating Molly's series of tests, who had slipped in unnoticed.

"I don't know if this is the miracle you are looking for or not, but we have found a possible physiological explanation for

Molly's mental lapses. At this point, I can't tell you if this is good news or bad. Thad, do you happen to know if she has fallen recently or had a blow to the head?"

"You know, I had completely forgotten that she took a pretty hard hit when our plane made that emergency landing. I think she had a slight concussion, but she insisted she was alright. Instead of wanting her injury seen about, she insisted on our helping those who she deemed worse off." Thad's countenance immediately mirrored his hope that God had granted Molly's miracle.

With Thankful Hearts

Two weeks later as Thad was driving Molly home from the hospital, he had been silent for several minutes. When Molly turned and looked at him, she saw why. Tears were raining down his face, but he had a gentle, peaceful expression.

Feeling that she knew the answer before she asked, Molly questioned, "Thad, I thought I received a near-perfect bill of health. What's the reason for those tears?"

"Molly, these are tears of joy and praise. I thought I was going to lose you to that mental abyss that swallows so many Alzheimer's patients. I can't quit thanking God we were wrong. I'm thanking God for a hematoma you received as a result of that lick on the head during the crash. I'll take a hematoma over that dreaded disease any day. And if you hadn't taken that wallop that caused the hematoma, that benign tumor pressing on your brain wouldn't have been found until it caused more problems, maybe irreparable damage."

"Oh, I thought you were crying because I made it through the surgery. But you can't get rid of me that easily," she teased.

"If God gives us five hundred more years together, I may get tired of you, but I doubt it. You can't imagine how much I love you and love having you by my side, mentally and physically. You were even sweet on your worst days. I will say, though, you made a pretty funny drunk after the surgery. It didn't take very much pain medication to make you loopy. I was glad when you were weaned off those, so I was assured that wasn't the new you. You gave us all a laugh the day you decided to take your gown off when the doctor came into the room."

"I did NOT do that. I would never do anything like that."

"Have it your way, but when the pictures Caitlin took surface, I will have my proof."

The mood of laughter continued for days and weeks afterward.

Although family and friends had been in abundance during her hospital stay, at Thad's suggestion, the remainder of the family and close friends gave them a few days and some space and time for Molly to rest and become reoriented to home. But the next weekend, they all had stayed away as long as they could. Caitlin, Bob, and Emily arrived first. Bob brought in a picnic basket filled with chicken and dumplings and a huge salad. Next, Celeste came in with her mom Gloria on the arm of the family friend, Sawyer Thomas, who had fallen for Gloria the first time they met. Celeste announced, "I brought my specialty – butter-pecan cake."

Before the door even closed, Benji stuck his head in and said, "Did I hear somebody say butter-pecan cake? I didn't come empty-handed either. I bought my specialty – a jug of Milo's sweet tea from the grocery store and rolls from the bakery."

Careful not to jar Molly's still-sore head, each in order, gave her a squeeze. Then Benji hugged her again. Trying to mask his tears of thanksgiving, he said, "Let's eat; I'm starved."

"And what's new about that?" laughed Caitlin.

When they gathered around the table, Benji said, "Celeste may have initiated the prayer for a miracle, but I'm gonna beat her to the draw in suggesting a family prayer of thanksgiving."

Bliss, For A While, At Least

Molly's recovery progressed at the speed of sound. Thad had great difficulty keeping her from rushing into the pace to which she was accustomed. "Molly, please, if for no other reason but to appease me, please, please slow down and give your body a chance to heal properly. I was so distressed when I thought I had lost you to Alzheimer's, I can't bear the thought of complications, and the surgery took its toll on your body. I just want nothing bad to happen to you for a hundred years or more."

"I promise I will try to rest more, but I'm so thankful for more life with you, I'm ready to get about living it. You know it is against my nature for others to serve me; I'd much rather do the serving."

"I know that, but think of it this way – you are stealing others blessings when you don't allow them to do for you."

Thad answered a call a few weeks later.

"After our wonderful meal at your house, I told you the next one was on me," Ralph Cochran said, without preamble. "I'm so sorry in being so long in getting back with you wonderful people, but things have been quite eventful since we last talked. Selina and I would like to take you to Atlanta for a special dinner. Would this coming Saturday night work for you two?"

After checking with Molly, Thad agreed they were free that night.

"We want to come, pick you up and drive there. This will give us more time to talk undisturbed. I must tell you though, I'm not sure you will recognize my family from what I had told you about them and how our lives' perspective is so different now. I want to tell you and show you what a vast difference Christ has made in our lives, but all of that will wait until we talk in person. By the way, our children will be with us too. We want you to meet the entire family. That's a big change that you could never fully understand because you didn't know us as a family before Christ transformed our home. Before, they would have been so disrespectful, we would have embarrassed for you to meet them. For the first time, we have a real family and a loving home, thanks to your influence and the grace of God."

"Are you two big meat lovers?" Ralph asked as they got into the car. "I hope so, because we have reservations at Fogo de Chao Brazilian Steakhouse. Have you ever eaten there?"

"Yes and no," answered Thad. "Yes, we both are big carnivores, and no, we haven't eaten there before, but when I attended a medical conference in Atlanta, some of the other doctors went one night and came back raving about it."

"It has become our special restaurant for celebrations. It's one that pleases everyone in the family," injected Selina.

Until that point in the conversation, Dahlia and Jackson, the Cochrans' teenage children, had sat in the third row of the Escalade not joining in the discussion. Dahlia spoke up when hearing they were going to her favorite restaurant. "Oh, great! I just love the gaucho waiters. Look, here it is on my IPad." She handed it a row up to the Simmons.

"That spit of meat looks scrumptious," said Thad. "And just look at the three-tiered salad bar, but I think it would be misnomer to call it a salad bar. Every vegetable imaginable is on it," added Molly.

"You don't want to fill up on that stuff though," commented Jackson, "because they just keep bringing meats of every kind to the table. I always save room for that."

"Jackson is most definitely our meat eater," added Selina. "I'm sorry you won't get to meet our oldest, Thomas. He's working tonight, but when he comes, the restaurant has to kill another cow."

"Yes, he's just one of the results of our changed lives. On his own, he decided he should get a part-time job to earn his own spending money while he's in college. I would have never believed it until it happened, but he doesn't see me as just a money tree anymore since Christ is number one in our lives," said Ralph.

"The next thing you know, Dad will throw Dahlia and me into the job market," joked Jackson. "When he does, I'm going to call the child labor folks on him."

"Now that's just not going to happen, at least until I get out of high school," said Dahlia, appalled at the thought.

"Did you notice how quiet it was in the back seat until the discussion of food started? I think that woke them up," laughed Ralph.

"I love it," said Molly. "Jackson, your sense of humor is so much like our son Benji's."

The remainder of the night was filled with gaiety and delightful conversation. In turn, each of the Cochrans shared their conversion experience with Thad and Molly. They commented on how they saw the world through different eyes, not just in a materialistic way.

"I know I would be in jail by now if all this hadn't reformed our family," commented Jackson. "I had already spent some nights in juvie for drugs and theft," he added, none too proudly.

"I lost my crowd of friends when I changed, but it really wasn't a loss at all. I now see how shallow they are – as we were," inserted Dahlia. "I'm surrounded by good people from my youth group and church now, and I've never been happier, even though my other friends have given up on me. They think I'm a freak or something because I go to church now."

Selina spoke up. "Yes, we've all changed more than you can imagine. We aren't perfect and are still growing in Christ, but thanks be to God, we're not where we once were. I've quit modeling and am a full-time mom; I'm cooking and actually eating real food. I decided being emaciated wasn't all it was cracked up to be." Selina laughed. "But I do still exercise. Our focus now is staying healthy. Ralph has started jogging with me. We have time to talk more that way. That's not something we ever did before, nor did we have any desire to share our days with each other."

"You mean, when I can breathe, I jog. She works me so hard, I can't say much, but I do listen to her."

In a more serious tone, Thad remarked, "Cochran, when you started to leave our house the night you gave your life to Christ, you were somewhat apprehensive about sharing this with Selina and the children. How did you broach the subject?"

"I didn't. I thought about it and decided I had to show them the difference it made in my life instead of telling them. I found a church nearby, and to their dismay, I would get up on Sunday morning and go. I also attended bible study one night a week. In it, I found a mentor, Jake Mynard. He helped me grow in my journey. It didn't take long for Selina to recognize a difference in the way I responded to her and the children and a transformation in the way I made time for the family. She's the one who raised the issue. She asked what happened to the old Ralph. I wanted to tell her, but I wanted to present the plan of salvation correctly. I brushed off her question until I could practice what I would say. Then to be sure I did it correctly, I asked Jake to come over and listen in. I wanted him to correct me if I got off tract. When Selina said she wanted what I had, we prayed together and she accepted Christ."

"Then my wild children began questioning my transformation. At first they thought I had lost my mind. I heard them ask Selina one day if she thought I had had a mental breakdown or something because I was so different." Ralph chuckled. "I thought that was a great compliment."

"By that time, my confidence was strong enough that I was able to tell them the ABC's myself."

In unison from the back seat came, "A – Admit you are a sinner; B –Believe in the Lord Jesus Christ; C – Confess with your mouth that God has saved you."

"And we can quote the scriptures for each letter too, if you want us to. Our Sunday school teacher drills us on these each week," added Dahlia.

"Yeah, to begin with, we thought our dad had died in the crash and someone else came home in his body," teased Jackson. Then in a more somber mood, he added, "Thank you, we like this dad much better. He even acts like he likes us now."

"It just might be that you are much more likeable now," answered their dad with a refreshing humor.

"We didn't do anything; this all came from on-high," said Molly.

The meal delivered everything the Cochrans had promised. "I've eaten in quite a few nice restaurants in my day," said Thad, as he pushed back from the table, "but I believe this one tops them all in quantity, as well as food quality and succulence."

"I should have worn old women's elastic-waisted pants," joked Molly, "because I'm sure I'm about to pop a button. I know I've sinned by eating so much tonight."

"I think God will forgive you for one night of gluttony, darling. You usually eat like a bird."

"I should have stopped with that gorgeous vegetable bar, but I didn't want to hurt the gaucho's feelings when they kept offering me slices of meat," Molly laughed.

When the Cochrans drove Thad and Molly home, Thad commented, "I don't think I've ever eaten so much in all my life, but I wanted to try everything. What was it? – three kinds of steak, pork tenderloin, lamb, chicken, and the list just goes on and on."

"And just for your information, Jackson, I did eat the vegetables from the salad bar. They were a gourmet delight, just as the meat was. I think we have consumed our weekly requirement for protein and veggies in one night." Molly laughed and added, 'Would you folks come in for some coffee?"

"Let's do that another night," answered Ralph. "It's getting late and I need to get home and waddle in the house."

"Just one more thing then," added Molly. "When we have our family gatherings, and they are often, you will be invited because we have grafted you into our family."

"Okay, Mom," Selina replied with exaggerated emphasis. "We will certainly do that, but I have one request."

"What is that, dear?"

"I want to come and help you cook so I can learn some of your gourmet tricks. Ralph wants our dinner table to look like yours." That ended the evening with joined laughter.

Another Connection

Being with the Cochrans brought back more memories of that horrific crash and the people they met to both Thad and Molly. They sat side-by-side in their easy chairs, not only recounting the events of the evening, but also discussing the trauma they shared in the accident. "You do realize just how blessed we were to come out of that wreckage alive, don't you?" Thad said.

"I do indeed. Life takes so many unexpected turns and I couldn't help but ask God that night if He was playing some kind of cruel joke on the two of us. We had found so much happiness with each other and were having the time of our life. I thought He was about to end it for us just as we were beginning our life together. I often think of those who were much less fortunate than we were."

"The one I think about the most often is Maliki," said Thad. "She had such a future ahead of her and was so excited to be traveling to Auburn to be on the swim team there. A person's plans and hopes can be destroyed in just a second."

"Thad, that's so strange you mentioned her. I had her on my mind just today. I often speak her name to Jesus, asking him to give her a new lease on life, but I really don't even know if she survived. But I have to believe she did. Why else would God put her on my mind so often? Is there any way we could find out? I know with the privacy act and all, it's harder to trace anyone's medical journey."

"It would be difficult, but let me do some research tomorrow and see what leaves I might overturn. I do know several of the orthopedic surgeons at Georgia Baptist. In the meantime, let's call it a night. I'm tired and know you must be exhausted. Our night with the Cochran's was fun, but I'm about through for one day. Darling, I love you for so many reasons, but one is the way you endear yourself to so many people. You are so easy for people to open up and talk with."

"You know me too well, Thad. I was about to suggest we call a close to this wonderful day. I'm so thankful God graced me with a husband so dedicated to Him." Hand in hand, they went up the stairs to their bedroom.

The next morning, Thad found Molly in her favorite place – the back patio. "You really enjoy having your coffee back here, don't you, darling? I often wonder what's going on in that sweet head of yours as you peer into the distance."

"I mainly reflect on the many blessings God has showered me with, you being at the top of that list."

Thad bent down and gave her an affectionate peck on top of her head. "I cherish you more every day, Molly. I not only love you deeply, but I respect your unwavering walk with the Lord. I just came out, not to interrupt your reverie, but to let you know what I found out about Maliki."

"Joseph Stern, head of orthopedics at Georgia Baptist, said he remembers her well. He said she had quite a battle in her recovery, which is still ongoing. He said in spite of all medical opinions that her leg should be amputated; she was resolute in her decision to keep it. She said, 'If you remove my leg, just kill me because I don't want to live without it.'"

"He went on to say that infections and many surgeries trying to put the pieces back together had almost cost Maliki her life. "She was a fighter though. She is now free of infections and is working fervently in rehab to get back use of her leg. She says she will eventually get to Auburn to compete on the swim team. Brett Hawke and the rest of the coaches and staff from Auburn have played a significant role in her recovery. Someone from the staff visits every week. They assure her that there will be a place for her there when she recovers. Her long-term goal is to swim in the Olympics."

"Thad, you are well aware that attitude often goes far beyond what surgeries and medicines can do," Molly interjected.

"He went on to say he would tell her of our prayers and concerns. Although he couldn't give me her contact info, he said the next time she was in his office he would suggest she get in touch with us and give her our number."

A couple of weeks later, the home phone rang after dinner. Molly got to it first. "Simmons residence; Molly speaking."

A tremulous voice on the other end said, "I'm not sure you remember who I am, but I met you on the plane. I'm Maliki."

"Oh, sweet Maliki, I certainly remember you. Dr. Thad and I haven't ceased praying for you since the paramedics whisked you away the day of the accident, although we weren't even sure you survived those catastrophic injuries. Please catch us up. How are you?"

"It has been a really rough year, but things are getting better. I guess the injury and trauma blocked my memory of everything that happened for a while. But, when I saw Dr. Stern this week for my check up, he said I had friends who had inquired about me. When he told me a little about you,

I started recalling what happened before our rough landing. I feel remiss in not trying to find you before, because you were such a comfort and strength for me."

"I wasn't sure you would ever recall any of it. God has a way of blocking many harrowing events from our minds. Are you still in rehab in Atlanta?"

"Oh, yes, and will be for quite some time yet. If it hadn't been for the staff and swim coaches at Auburn, I couldn't have remained here and got the treatment I have. Fortunately, they had me sign insurance forms before I left Bermuda. They also have been my surrogate family through this ordeal. There's no way my birth family could have afforded coming here, but the coaches even set me up where I could have face time with them via the internet."

"Mailiki, would you be up to Dr. Thad and me driving to Atlanta to visit you and catch up face-to-face?"

"I would love that. Could you come next week?"

Molly could hear the excited little girl in her voice. She knew the child must have been so lonely. "We will definitely see you next week. I will call to confirm the time and day after I discuss it with Dr. Thad."

When Molly reported her discussion with Maliki to Thad, he pondered all she said for a few minutes and then said, "Molly, I have an idea, and I think God just gave it to me. He has blessed us abundantly in many ways, even financially. We agreed early in our marriage that everything we are, everything we have is to be used for His glory. Why don't we arrange a visit for Maliki's parents? I believe being with them would be better than therapy or medicine. She still has a long road ahead of her. Maybe this will give her the impetus to continue."

"Oh Thad, that is a great idea. We can get contact information from her when we see her next week. Every day God shows me more reasons to love you."

Celebration Turns Bad

After their exhilarating visit with Maliki and sharing with her their plans to bring her parents to see her, they returned home and called the family to tell them how God had worked in still another spectacular way.

"Thad, I can't believe just how fast time flies by. It seems only days since we celebrated Emily's birth, and now we are going to Atlanta to celebrate her fifth birthday. Caitlin wants us to stay over after the party until the next day and go with them to the Memorial Day parade. She says Emily is totally exuberant about seeing the band and soldiers marching by."

Atlanta's streets were filled with excited families awaiting the big parade. For a while Bob let Emily ride on his shoulders so she would have a better view of the happenings. When she spotted her good friend Ivy, a neighborhood friend, she was too embarrassed to stay on her dad's shoulders because she thought that made her look like a baby. "I want down; I want to walk," she told Bob.

"Okay, but you need to hold somebody's hand so we won't get separated." She clutched his hand tightly until she spotted a man making balloon animals. After she broke loose to run to get one, the rest of the family stopped at the street vendor just steps away to buy hot dogs and cokes. With four adults in the group, surely one of them had an eye on Emily. NO.

In the blink of an eye, the beautiful five-year-old had vanished. Trying to avoid panic, they separated to start circling the immediate area. Surely she had just found something close by to investigate. Making larger and larger circles to no avail, alarm then set in. Bob lost his normal reserve and started yelling at the top of his lungs, "Emily, Emily, where are you?'

Upon hearing her dad's call, Emily started responding with her own yell, but was stopped with the strong hand of the stranger across her mouth muffling the sound. "You can't be loud, sweetie, you'll scare the puppies." Puppies that Emily had yet to see, the ones the stranger had said he wanted to show her.

Never go anywhere with a stranger. These words of caution echoed in Emily's mind as she began feeling uncomfortable in the dark van with this strange, smelly man. Guilt filled her heart because of her disobedience.

Caitlin couldn't say anything because of her sobbing. Molly, trying to comfort her, said, "We will find her soon; I know we will. Let's ask God to help us find her."

"Mom, what if she has been kidnapped?" voiced Emily in jerky sobs. That had been the unspoken fear of the entire family. In just minutes, other families, seeing the terror, joined in the search.

Thad proved to be the steady force in the group. "We need you to stay right here by where the balloon man had been, Molly, in case she finds her way back here. The rest of us need to separate and go in different directions looking for her and asking if anyone has seen her. Bob, you find a policeman and report her missing. Give him our cell phone numbers in case they find her. Look at your watches. Call Molly every ten minutes to see if anyone has found her."

Three hours of searching had turned up nothing. By then, the crowd had started to disperse. "Maybe she will be easier to find when the crowd breaks up," the mounted policeman told the group who had reassembled. "Don't lose heart, I know we will find her," he said in a not-so-convincing tone. Officer Tonelli felt the family's pain because he had three preschoolers himself. "If she doesn't appear soon, we will send out an Amber alert."

By then, street lights started coming on, and the search seemed hopeless. Tonelli finally instructed the family to return to the house where they could be contacted if there were any developments. Reluctantly, the group started toward the parking lot, when they heard the sound of running hooves on the pavement. When they looked up, they all were overcome with joy when they saw the prettiest site ever. There was Emily in front of a policeman sitting astride the horse. She was laughing and enjoying the ride, for to ride a real horse had been one of her birthday wishes. But as she neared her family, the waterworks began. She shed tears of remorse for her disobedience and for causing her family such distress.

"I heard someone might be looking for this birthday girl," said Officer Snell. "She seemed to have strayed off as she followed a clown down the street."

Hugs and kisses abounded, as the child was returned. The officer watched the reunion and then called Bob and Emily aside. "It wasn't quite as innocent as we presented. This clown had already been reported for luring children away. We had been looking for him for an hour, when another officer reported seeing him enticing a little girl in a van. Fortunately, she was rescued just after stepping in. I believe someone must have been praying. Not all these incidents end this well."

An Unexpected Vacation

Weeks passed and the busyness of life overshadowed their great celebration of a family reunited.

Bob and Caitlin experienced some significant marital problems after Emily was born. Bob's workaholic tendencies kept him for being there for Caitlin when she experienced postnatal depression. Her suicide attempt gave him quite a jolt and a vivid wake-up call. After some intense marriage therapy, they grew much closer than they had ever been.

After several years, they moved into a comfortable love-filled routine. But time and circumstances gradually took their toll and sucked at this renewed passion until it was just a drip. The sexual fire didn't die, but it reduced to a slow simmer. Every day responsibilities and tedium took its place. They both seemed satisfied with the status quo. They agreed this was still better than a stormy relationship.

But Bob soon sensed that revitalization was badly needed in their waning yearnings. One day he came in beaming, "Caitlin, I have a surprise for you. We are going to take that long-needed vacation, just the two of us."

In a non-stop excited chatter, Caitlin asked, "Where? When? I love the idea, but I need details. The last time we discussed going somewhere besides to our folks, we agreed we didn't have the extra funds for such non-essentials. Who will care for Emily?"

Laughing at her exuberance, Bob interjected, "Whoa, girl. Come up for air and I will tell you. Mr. Jacobs, our company's CEO, called me in today and gave me an excellent mid-year evaluation." With an ear-to-ear smile, he thumbed out his lapel and added, "He told me what an asset I've been, and he said that kind of work needed to be rewarded."

With an exaggerated prissy air, Caitlin said, "Well, aren't you the cat's meow?" She grabbed his lapels and pulled him down to give him a kiss. "I'm so proud of you." Then jumping up and down like a child, she said, "But I want to know about the trip."

"Wow! With a response like that of just the news of a trip, I can't wait for your reaction when we actually get there." He pulled her into a close embrace and they locked with a romantic kiss. When they came up for air Bob continued, "I had expected a nice raise, which I'm getting, but he said there was more. He has a luxurious three-story beach house on Palm Island and is giving us the use of it for a week next month. He said he would even have his guide to bring his boat from the marina for us to fish as often as we like."

Still bubbling with joy, Caitlin said, "I don't know about fishing, but spending a day on the water sounds so relaxing."

Bob hadn't seen this gleam in Caitlin's eyes in years. She was totally giddy. He asked, "Do you think your mom and Thad would keep Emily for us so we can be entirely free of responsibility?"

"I feel certain they will because Mom is always telling me that you and I need to get away, just the two of us. I know Emily is going to want to go too, but maybe Mom and Thad will do something special with her during that time to make up for our going without her." Then showing some hesitation Caitlin said, "But there is so much to do here. I am scheduled to host our small group, make a cake for our charity cake bake, and ..." Caitlin continued naming over general responsibilities and things on the calendar that conflicted with the dates.

"Caitlin, just listen to yourself. These are the things that are taking over our lives, things that bring such busyness into our everyday existence that we no longer have time for us. We need a total break from all of this, for a while anyway. These things can easily be cancelled or rescheduled."

"I know, I know. I hear what you're saying, and you're right. I'll start tomorrow making calls and clearing our schedule. I am really excited, Bob. You are the best husband ever."

The next weeks flew by like a comet. Even packing for the trip was thrilling, and the anticipation of getting away already had made the two more romantic. Emily held up a sexy teddy she hadn't worn in years. *I think this will add a little pizzazz to the trip.* She folded it and tucked it in the suitcase with some of the other pieces of lingerie she had bought just for the occasion. As they drove to Palm Island, their favorite songs played on the CD player. Stevie Wonder's *I Just Called to Say I Love You,* Whitney Houston's *Saving All My Love For You,* and other love songs from their play list resounded with their feelings for each other.
Singing along like they did when they were dating as they made the drive, confirmed they were getting into a relaxed mood already.

Upon arriving, they drove onto the ferry, the only access to the island. "Say, 'Goodbye, world.' We won't be going back to the mainland for a week, so I hope you have everything you need. Jacobs said he would have the fridge stocked with all our food stuffs."

When the GPS led them to the address, Caitlin's eyes widened. "This can't be right; this isn't a house; it's a mansion."

"Yep, this is it. One of the other guys in the firm had already told me about it. He said the outside paled in comparison to the inside."

"Well, hurry up. Let's go in and check it out." Caitlin couldn't rein in her enthusiasm. She ran in and explored every nook and cranny. "Bob, are we in Heaven?"

"Not quite, but I think we will be before the night is over, babe." He took her in his arms with the affection that had been missing lately. Sure enough, after grilling the steaks that had been left for them and adding the great sides, the couple enjoyed a relaxed dinner. Looking out over the gigantic, inviting pool, with a gleam in her eyes mixed with a tad of mischievous, Caitlin said, "Let's go for a midnight swim."

"That's a superb idea. We're completely alone, so we won't even have to go up for our swimsuits; we can strip and just jump in. Just another nod to our freedom this week," interjected Bob.

Caitlin raised an eyebrow and teased, "I think you are just a lecherous old man, but," adding with glee, "I like it." She was so ready. "On my count we hit it. One, two, three."

The liberty to be children instead of being encapsulated with the responsibility of being the parents was totally exhilarating. After an hour of playing and flirting like teenagers, they decided it was time to call it a night, so they headed up the winding stairs to their massive suite.

They slept until midmorning. Slowly stretching and opening her eyes to the bright sunlight, Catlin announced she was famished. A few minutes later, they sat at the breakfast nook feasting on muffins and fruit, still a touch drunk from the night of pleasure they had enjoyed. Still in their robes, they were startled by a rap on the bay window where they sat. Waving and walking toward the back door was the most fetching creature Caitlin had ever laid eyes on. The man let himself in after punching the combination he had known for several years. He walked to the table and picked up a muffin as though he belonged there.

"Hi, I'm Scotty Tanner, your fishing guide. Mr. Jacobs told me to have the boat ready for you and take you out today. Time's a wasting. I have the bait and gear in the boat. Get dressed and let's go catch some big ones."

Caitlin sat frozen with her flimsy robe clutched together to hide her nakedness underneath. She was mesmerized by this tan, muscular man standing near her and was very aware of her state of undress.

Standing up quickly, Bob introduced himself and Caitlin. "We'll be ready shortly." He reached back a hand for Caitlin who was reluctant to stand up in her sheer robe.

Turning to her, Scotty said, "Don't waste time on hair or make up. You don't need it and it would be useless on the boat anyway."

Upstairs as they threw on some shorts and tees, Bob laughed and commented, "Caitlin, I thought you were going to attack our guide before we even got to know him. You just about undressed him with your eyes."

"I did not; I was so shocked he caught me in this state," blushing, she denied. "But if I did, it was because I didn't think I needed to be the only one naked." Then in keeping with jovial mood, she added, "But he is eye-candy, don't you think?"

With that, Bob playfully swatted her on the rear. "You've been a very bad girl on this trip, and I like it – a lot."

As they skimmed across the water, Caitlin sat near the front of the boat and enjoyed the sun warming her pale skin and the wind blowing her hair. Caitlin had not felt this care-free since she was a teenager; not even then because she lived in the house with an overbearing, strict preacher dad.

"Did you lather on sunscreen before we left?" checked Scotty. "Here is some that won't stain the boat and the fish don't smell it," he added as he tossed the tube to her. "I would hate for that white skin to burn." The night before had rekindled desires in her she had thought were lost forever. Scotty's even noticing her to that extent caused a surprised stir in her.

When she handed it back, she was aware when his rough hand touched hers. He sent the tube Bob's way unaware of the electricity Caitlyn had experienced. Since Bob was sitting at the back of the boat, verbal communication was all but impossible with the roar of the motor and the slapping of the waves. But Catlin noticed Bob's peaceful, unstressed demeanor. This trip was truly a Godsend for them both.

After the boat came to a stop out in the ocean, Bob, who was already a seasoned fisherman, took the rig Scotty passed to him and cast out. Scotty passed a baited rig to Caitlin.

"I don't fish. I just came for the ride," she said as she threw her hands back as though the fishing rod would bite.

"Well, you do starting today," Scotty insisted as he almost forced the rod in her hands. She stood staring at it as though it were a snake. "Don't worry; I'll show you, young lady. I'm a great teacher."

His commanding, light-hearted manner, made Caitlin stand ready for instructions. Her first attempt was a total disaster, leaving the gear in a snarled nest. "I'm so sorry," she said embarrassed.

"No problem; I just have to do more showing than telling for you, but wait a minute while I help this professional fisherman back here bring in his catch. He's got a big one."

Sure enough, Bob had caught a huge grouper.

"Now bringing in dinner makes me feel like a real man," Bob quipped. Turning to Scotty who had expertly netted it for him, he added with a wink, "What do you think my chances are for getting Caitlin to clean and filet it?"

"I'd say slim-to-none," Scotty answered with an ear to ear smile as he looked back to the pristine slender blonde who still was perfectly clean in her white shorts and matching tank top."

At dusk, they headed in. The glimmering sun setting on the water was mesmerizing. Although the sun and surf had exhausted both Caitlin and Bob, they were perfectly tranquil. Because the temperature was dropping and the wind chilled her, Caitlin slipped on her denim over-shirt. Bob noticed that and moved up to where she was sitting. He put his arm around her and drew her close. After about thirty minutes, they pulled up to the pier. The couple sat still for a few moments as they were enthralled by the beauty of the sun setting into the water.

Scotty unloaded the boat and skillfully filleted the fish in mere minutes. "I'll be back about the same time tomorrow, so have some clothes on this time," he laughed. He noticed and smugly enjoyed the blush rising in Caitlin's cheeks.

Caitlin's Fling

Together, the two prepared a simple meal of baked fish, baked potatoes, and salad. After settling in front of the TV and enjoying a romantic movie, they started upstairs, only to be stopped by the ringing of Bob's phone. They looked at each other in surprise. He was off-the-clock, and they were hoping it wasn't a problem with Emily. Caitlin could surmise by listening to Bob's side of the conversation that it was someone from the office. "Yes, definitely I want to be there. What happened – a heart attack? Give me those details again so I can write them down. Uh huh, I'll leave in the morning. No, no. I would have been upset if you hadn't called me. Coming back for the service is just the right thing to do. I'll fly back to Atlanta and then back here the next day."

When the conversation ended, Bob explained to Caitlin that one of his bosses, Larry McClellan, died from a sudden heart attack. "I will go for the funeral tomorrow and come back the next day. This shouldn't interfere with your stay. With the alarm system, I think you will be perfectly safe. I wouldn't leave but I think I'm expected to be there or they wouldn't have notified me. The company is even taking care of my flights."

"I'll be fine and will enjoy some alone time. You know, I never have that."

The next morning, Caitlin heard that same tap at the bay window. When Scotty came in, she said, "Oh, I'm so sorry. Bob had to leave for an office emergency early this morning. We should have called you."

"Why's that? Just because he's not here doesn't mean you can't go out. Anyway, this way I can give you my undivided attention and make a real fisherwoman out of you."

"I don't know. Maybe we should just cancel going out for today."

"I'll not hear of it. Wash that muffin down and let's wet a hook."

Caitlin was aware of her strong attraction to Scotty, but tried to ignore it. He had seemed to be oblivious to it. He was very attentive helping her onto the boat and getting her settled in the seat beside his. "If you ride here, the windshield will protect you from some of the spray. The water is rougher today than it was yesterday, but we will be okay." Before they got out far, the strong surf would make it impossible for her not to fall into Scotty occasionally. He was grounded by holding the steering wheel. By the time they reached their destination, accidental contact had turned to laughter. Finally, he put his strong arm around her and held her close to him to prevent her from falling from the seat. When they finally stopped, he kept holding her. Both remained silent for several minutes.

Scotty's demeanor changed. So did his conversation. "Caitlin, this is the first time I have held another woman like that since my wife died five years ago. I must say I enjoyed it."

"My wife Susie and I met in college and married after graduation. She taught first-grade and was good at it. I was a professor of math at Georgia Tech, our alma mater. With busy careers, we never got around to having the children we had hoped for. She was the love of my life and my encourager, supporter, lover and much more. Shortly after our eighth anniversary, Susie was diagnosed with stage four colon cancer. Chemo and radiation did little to help."

Caitlin observed the trance-like stare and the sadness in Scotty's magical blue eyes. She realized he was in a world of his own right then, although his arm was still around her.

"Maybe it gave her another year, but a torturous one at that. We were what I would say nominal Christians, attending church maybe three or four times a year. After I had prayed fervently for her healing, I saw those prayers weren't being answered the way I wanted them to be. I was angry with God and with the world. I felt my faith faltering. I just wanted to get away. That's when I resigned my position and bought a small place here. Finally, I knew I couldn't stew in the broth of anger and grief forever, and I realized I had to busy myself with something. That's when I bought a boat and used the skills my dad had taught me as a young boy as a fishing guide. It got me out on the water where I found some degree of peace, and I started regaining my faith; I knew only a good God could make a world so beautiful and that his ways were beyond my comprehension. That's about it." Scotty tried to inconspicuously wipe a tear away that had found its way halfway down his tanned cheek.

Caitlin was curious about this man. "I don't know much about you. Tell me more about Susie and yourself."

Scotty recounted many memories. It was though many of the depressed details of Susie's illness and death had been stored in some hidden place and were eager to unfold. After emptying himself of things he had held tightly for so long, he realized he had done all the talking. "I'm so sorry I've rattled on and told you more than you ever wanted to hear. Tell me about you and Bob."

"No, no. I wanted to hear all about you. I think you may have needed to tell some of this too." Then Caitlin started unfolding much of her story. Rather than fishing, Scotty sat enthralled as Caitlin poured out more information to him than she ever had to anyone but Bob. After an hour of talking about her parents, her dad's spiritual fall, his crippling accident and his ultimate death, her postpartum depression after Emily's birth leading to her suicide attempt, she blurted out information that should never have been discussed with anyone but Bob – the ho-humness of their relationship as of late and other intimate details, even about how their love-life had taken on a fresh start since they had been at Palm Island and how she had learned a freedom she had not known before in their lovemaking.

There was something about their individual hurts and joys that drew them to each other. Scotty embraced her tightly and whispered, "I'm so sorry you have had so many hurts."

"Me, too. I know losing one you loved so dearly was hard for you, Scotty."

Neither of them said much more as they stared into the setting sun's orange reflection on the blue water. As they arrived at the pier, Scotty tied the boat off, and the two walked into the house, arm-in-arm. The mutual attraction was undeniable. Without a word, Scotty led her upstairs to the bedroom. Caitlin went willingly.

Catlin's Regrets

After basking in heavy petting and compelling desire, it was Scotty who came to his senses. He hopped out of bed and said, "Caitlin, we can't do this. I won't do this. You have a husband who loves you and a child who will look to you as a life's role model. Although I find you beautiful and alluring, I know this is wrong. Please make excuses to Bob for me. Tell him I had a family emergency or something and can't finish out the week."

Caitlin lay with a sheet over her totally aghast. Shame immediately overtook her as she realized, except for Scotty's resistance, she would have fallen the same way her dad had and would have hurt people just as he had. She buried her face into the pillow crying out to God for forgiveness. How could she have been overtaken with passion? She had even had a holy nudge when they sat with Scotty's arm around her, that she should break this bodily contact. She hadn't though. Why had she encouraged it? How black with sin she felt! How could she ever face Bob again?

The next morning, Caitlin pulled herself up after a restless night. When she looked in the mirror, she saw some woman with swollen eyes she didn't even like. She fell to her knees right there in the bathroom, and in great anguish cried out to God. "Oh, Father, I have sinned against you and Bob. I am a wretched sinner. I am so weak to have let temptation overtake me like that. Please, in your mercy, please forgive me. What can I do, God? Should I confess to Bob what I have to you?"

Call your mom, seemed to be the answer calling out to her. She knew there was nothing she could do that would be so bad her mom would quit loving her; then she realized the same thing about God. She wasn't so sure about Bob though.

Call to Molly

Caitlin thought her mom was invincible and always had the answer to any problem. Although she had butted heads with her many times as a teenager, she now appreciated her great wisdom. She grew impatient and fearful as the phone rang four, then five times. *What if she's not home? I don't think I can make it if I don't talk to her now.* Caitlin knew her mom rarely turned her cell phone on. She was not one tied to technology. Just as Caitlin was about to give up, the voice mail message was interrupted with Molly's breathless hello.

"Mom, I'm so glad you answered," said a tearful Caitlin.

"I had been out in the garden and heard the phone just as I was just coming in. I had to wash the dirt from my hands before I could answer. What's wrong? Are you crying, dear?"

For a minute, Caitlin couldn't reply. At last, she regained her composure enough to speak. "Mom, I've messed up so badly, I'm not sure you can even love me again."

Molly, shocked by what Caitlin was saying, replied, "Caitlin, you could rip my heart out and stomp on it, and I would still love you. You know that, darling. Please tell me this terrible thing you've done that would make you say that."

"Mom, I've sinned so-o-o bad. You know how hard it was for me to forgive Dad of his unfaithfulness to you. I hated him for so long. I condemned him. Now, I am no better than he was." She went on to recount the joys of their vacation, how Bob had to go back home for a while, and then how she was overtaken with temptation and lust. She described in great detail the entire scenario. "Mom, if it had not been for Scotty coming to his senses I would have gone all the way. I had no intention of putting on the brakes. I was already giving in completely. I feel I've committed adultery. I've confessed and repented to God. Now, I want to tell you how sorry I am."

"Oh, Caitlin, you know I love you, regardless. We ALL have sinned."

"Hmm, Mom, you've never even had a lustful thought. Any sin you may have committed would be so minor, compared to mine. Mom, do you think I've inherited Dad's sexual weakness? I'm no better than he was, and we condemned him so for his fall, all except for you. You were so quick and willing to forgive him."

"Caitlin, now you are letting Satan take you down the wrong thought process. You can't blame your sin on your father. You were doing it right when you were in the simple repentant mode. Don't play the blame game. We each have to claim our own sins. We all have temptations. Maybe mine aren't the same as yours, but, believe me, I do have temptations. "

"Mom, I can't wrap my mind around the fact that the devil could ever tempt you in any way. You are so strong in your faith."

"Well, dear, this isn't the time for me to recount the many times I've had unholy desires because this is about you right now."

"But Mom, I'm not so sure Bob will ever forgive me. What am I to do?"

After a long pause, Molly said, "Listen to me closely. I'm not sure you need to tell Bob. Let me explain my reasoning. It was so important to confess to God and receive His forgiveness. I know it would relieve a burden of your guilt if you come clean with Bob, but that guilt may be a burden you have to bear. Sin always exacts a price. Even though it might absolve you, think of the damage it would do to Bob, to your family if he knew. I don't approve of lying or not sharing things with your husband, but this time you must think of the greater good."

"But Mom, he will be back here soon. How can I face him?"

"You pay your sin debt by being the most loving and devoted wife you can possibly be for the rest of your life. If you will allow Him to, God will make something beautiful from this darkest hour. This is our secret forever."

A Time of Thanksgiving

Molly had prayed daily that Caitlin would do as she had suggested and that she would be a better wife to Bob than she ever had. After she had seen them together several times since, she felt her prayers had been answered. They showed more outward expressions of love and adoration than they ever had.

One day Molly had an epiphany. "Thad, we don't have to wait until November to have a Thanksgiving celebration, you know. With the way God has been with us through so many crises this year, I would like to gather the family and have a special 'Thank you, Jesus' celebration."

"I think you are spot on with that idea, Molly. Our pastor said only Sunday, 'What if God provides for you tomorrow only what you've thanked God for today.'" I know we have all thanked him privately for the times he has brought beauty from ashes, but a family celebration for these things would be ideal."

"You think the children will think I'm losing it again when I invite them for Thanksgiving in the middle of August?" giggled Molly. "They'll line me up for the loony bin, for sure. I can just imagine Benji's comments."

"I believe they will simply be learning from their mother how to show glory to God through the good days and bad. You know what? I think we should include the Cochrans in this celebration since one thing we are thankful for is that God used a plane crash to bring them to the Lord."

"What a great idea! You know me, the more, the merrier. I hope Benji can get here from school. I know his studies keep him busy, but maybe we can plan it during a long weekend."

Thad and Molly began making a list of the things they wanted to be included in their thanksgiving: God's saving them during the plane disaster; the opportunity to share the gospel with the Cochrans; Molly's successful brain surgery and the good news she didn't have Alzheimer's; finding Emily safe; and Benji's acceptance to University of Georgia. Molly had other unspoken thank-you's.

"There's one other thing I'd like to include," said Thad. "The life God is letting us share together may need to go to the top of the list." He reached out and took her into a strong embrace, looked deep into her dreamy eyes, and planted a lingering kiss on her cotton candy lips.

When she regained her composure she replied, "I couldn't agree more. I am truly the happiest I have ever been in my life," With tears of joy streaming down her beaming face, she lay her head on his strong chest.

Little did they know their family and friends would find themselves in the midst of another life-threatening crisis the next day at the most unusual place.

A Devil Amonst Us

One of the greatest joys in Molly's life was to have her entire family at church worshipping together. She beamed with pride as she gazed up and down the bench on Sunday, seeing her sweet family gathered once again on the same pew in the same church where they had every Sunday when they were growing up. One of the first Bible verses she taught them was Psalm 122:1 - *I was glad when they said unto me, Let us go into the house of the Lord.* It was never a question at Molly's house, "Are we going to church today?" That was not because they grew up in a pastor's home; it was because Molly loved the Lord and wanted to go to His house to worship Him and to instill in her children that same desire. The question still was never raised when the grown children came home. They knew to come prepared to go to church with their mom.

The music had changed since they were kids. Instead of all hymns, the minister of music was keeping up with the times and with changing musical appetites. He led in a blended service – some hymns, some praise songs, and he would even throw in some old gospel favorites occasionally.

The family had often discussed their preferences in music. The younger ones preferred praise music and the gospel style because those old songs were new to them, while the older members favored hymns. Thad had said at one time that he had a difficult time appreciating the praise songs because the same words were repeated so much. Benji had joked, "Thad, that's so you old folks can learn them and remember them."

Molly inserted, "The music style doesn't have to be according to my taste; if it praises God and keeps the younger generation engaged in worship, I refuse to be critical. It is about what brings glory to Him." That shut down that discussion because everyone realized she was right.

The entire family sang that day with nothing but the overflowing praise they felt in their hearts. Melanie Sisco, a close family friend, sang a solo that brought the congregation to their feet when she finished, not as an accolade to her, but in agreement to the words they could all identify with. *Because He Lives* held slightly different meanings for each person. On Molly's pew, each family member reflected on times they could not have gone on without the presence of the living Savior.

A holy hush fell over the congregation as Pastor Hull approached the pulpit. Just as he finished reading his text, a young man burst through a side entrance. His eyes were wild, his clothes looked as though he had slept for days in them, and his voice rang throughout the building. The worshipper's eyes were glued to the weapons he brandished in each hand, an automatic high-powered assault rifle in one, and an automatic revolver in the other. He had an ammunition belt across his chest that held enough bullets and shells to mow down every person in the place. He positioned himself in center, right in front of the pulpit.

To emphasize he meant business, he fired shots through the Wurlitzer baby grand on the stage. Bullets ricocheted, barely missing some front-row choir members. "Don't a-one of you try to be a hero. If you as much as move, you're dead on the spot. If I see a flash of light from a cell phone, these young children near the front will be the first victims." Nervousness was evident as he wiped sweat from his brow with his shirt sleeve. His extreme jumpiness and dilated pupils signaled he was high on drugs as well. "As a matter of fact, I think they will go first anyway. It will save them a lifetime of your propaganda. You are all infidels. I came here when I was young and believed all your sh---. Since I've converted to Islam, I realize how wrong you are. It will be my honor to die after I've mowed all of you down."

A plethora of thoughts passed through Caitlin's mind. *Have I brought this on my family and church by my sins? Is God going to punish us all because I still fantasize about my interlude with Scotty? Maybe I should have ignored Mom's advice and been forthcoming about my indiscretions with Bob. If I had, I might have been able to really have put all this out of my mind. Satan keeps putting ungodly thoughts in my head even if I live a façade of being the loving, devoted wife. God, if you will spare all of us today, I promise I will fall on my face every day and every night begging your forgiveness and asking you to help me to quit play-acting and really be the person to Bob I pretend to be. God, show me what I'm to do and how to do it.*

Molly got a glimpse of Benji, who was sitting near the end of the pew, and just knew from his posture and the glare in his eyes that he was primed to do something. He was as impetuous as was the disciple Peter. She knew it would mean disaster if he moved, not only for him, but also for others. She quietly cleared her throat to get his attention. Just with her expression and eye movement, he knew she was signaling him to stay put. He had seen such signals when he was much younger and had had the urge to do something untoward in church.

Not only did Benji hear his mother's signal, but so did this wild monster at the front. He swung both weapons in her direction and poised himself to shoot. Molly realized her life would be taken from her any moment. *Maybe that will divert his attention from those sweet children,* she thought. She closed her eyes in preparation for what was to come and silently prayed. *Dear God, if you are ready for my life here to be over, so be it, but please spare these children and others here.*

A shot rang out. Molly waited but felt no pain. *Is death this easy and painless?* she wondered. *Why do we all dread it so much?* Only when Thad put his arm around her and pulled her to him, did she realize she wasn't hit. She and the others were in awe when they saw their pastor with his own weapon. He had taken the man down with one shot in the back.

At the church's recent safety meetings, the committee had agreed they must be prepared in the event an intruder came in with the intent to harm. Even though the congregation was shocked to realize their pastor had kept a weapon on the shelf in the pulpit and was so skilled in using it, they would have been even more surprised to know just how many men in the congregation were also armed that day in the Lord's house. The decision had been to only fire a weapon if there was no other way. The pastor saw that if he didn't do something, Molly would definitely die on the spot and probably the children and many others would face the same fate. Being positioned behind the intruder gave him the best opportunity to bring the man down.

Even after the police arrived, Caitlin had found a spot away from the body at the edge of the altar. There, she poured her heart and mind out to the Lord. She not only thanked him for preserving the lives of her family and friends, but at last, really asked God to purge her of all unrighteousness. When she looked up, Bob was at her side with his arm around her. All she said to him was, "I'm so sorry."

As though intuitively he already knew, he squeezed her tightly and said, "All is forgiven. Say no more."

After long interrogations and statements given to law officials, the family returned home, somewhat in a state of shock. Words didn't come easily from any of them. Finally, Molly brought some levity to the situation when she snickered and covered her mouth to squelch even a greater laugh. "I think I had better go change my clothes; I think I peed my pants in fright."

Later than had been anticipated, Molly still laid a beautiful meal on the long table. "I know the events of today may have taken our appetites. I know; not yours, Benji. Just like our "Thanksgiving in August" meal a few years ago, we have much to be thankful for today. Only God could have intervened to have saved our lives."

"That, along with a pistol-packing pastor," Benji injected.

"The family ate their fill, in spite of the trauma of the day. Then the thank-you's were voiced, some Thad and Molly had anticipated; others that held special personal significance to each one there.

"While we are in this thankful mood, I would like to give a thank you for something that hasn't taken place yet." All eyes focused on Benji while they were trying to understand his meaning. "I want to thank God for going with me on my upcoming journey to Afghanistan." Audible gasps filled the silence.

"What are you saying, Benji?" He turned to his mom and gave her and the entire group Uncle Sam's plans for his next few years.

"I know I'm no better than anyone else who has been called up, and I do owe a debt of service for my scholarship. I don't want this to bring sadness, because I know God will be with me."

Ties That Break

Benji's almost four years of college seemed to have flashed by. During those years, he had enjoyed his basketball, although it had not been without trials, as well as pleasure. Basketball, along with his studies, had occupied most of his time and energy, which affected his relationship with his girlfriend Belinda.

"Benji, is our relationship ever going beyond where we are now? We've been dating exclusively since our freshman year. Here we are within two months of graduating, and it doesn't seem we have gone past where we were three years ago." Belinda had been in total agreement about no sex before marriage, but she had waited long enough for Benji to actually propose, not to talk about marriage in generalities.

Benji's heart swelled with both consuming love and horrifying dread as he watched his sweet Belinda wipe tears from her ocean-blue eyes. The sun was setting and a slight wind was swirling her long corn-silk hair back with a few stray strands circling her throat.

"You know how much I love you, don't you?" He looked into her eyes with sincere passion. "We've talked about marriage at a future time, but you want to know when. I understand that, but I've been waiting to see what Uncle Sam has in mind for my future." Benji touched her face and wiped a tear from her eye. "You know I owe the army four years for their paying my tuition and ROTC training. If I were going to be stationed at some stateside base, I had envisioned a wedding and living in base housing somewhere and maybe starting a family in a couple of years." Benji dropped his gaze to the ground. "I've dreaded telling you this, but the word came down last week that after a few weeks of basic training, we "newbies" will be deployed to some spot in the Middle East. The wheels have come off over there; the area is in total chaos. I just told my folks this past weekend. Although it isn't top secret, the President hasn't made it public that he is sending more units over, because bringing soldiers home has been a feather in his political cap. Sweetie, I simply don't know what our immediate future holds. I wish I knew."

"Benji, I've been patient long enough. I love you, but I'm not willing to keep waiting because I feel you will simply let something else interfere with our relationship after this. I should have seen the handwriting on the wall before this. I wish you well." Belinda reached up, ran a loving finger down his cheek, and turned and walked away. Benji didn't call after her.

You Can't Undo It

"You just can't undo some things," said the tall one-armed guy with an infectious smile. "You have to do the best you can with what you have. You'll find it more than sufficient to fulfill your life's purpose." His smile never faded as he looked down on Benji lying in the bed.

Benji had turned to face the wall. He hadn't wanted to hear any of the platitudes that had been offered by the therapist; he certainly didn't want to hear it from this doctor who had appeared in his room.

"You will find many in rehab much worse off than you," Sydney, the therapist had offered.

How dare him to throw that in my face. I'm not interested in other's sad stories. I'm just trying to make it through this day, and I really don't have much ambition beyond that. His life was over without his right leg. His dreams of being a pilot were dashed. He would never run on the basketball court and shoot hoops again. He would never even try to reconcile his differences with Belinda.

Now this new doctor appeared as though his words could fix things. He wasn't even one of his personal doctors.

92

Not even his mother's encouraging words had brought him out of his dungeon of depression. "Benji, you know the truth in the scripture from Romans about all things working for good to those who love the Lord and are called according to his purpose. God will work good through this, I know," His mom had comforted him many times before – when he was a kid with a skinned knee, when he lost basketball game and hadn't played his best game, when his dad had been too rough on him – but this wasn't a skinned-knee moment.

He had not even found it in himself to be gracious to her. "I'm not you, Mom. I can't take your Pollyanna outlook. And the good that God can work – is this just another of His evil tests to see how strong I am? I think too much testing must come from a cruel God. Just don't talk to me about Him right now, okay? He and I aren't on such good terms at this moment," he had lashed out at the woman he had always admired, but now, resented. "Why don't you go home? I'll call you when I'm ready to see you again. I've got to sort through this by myself and just can't take, nor do I want, sympathy or pep talks. Words can't give me back my leg."

In the way that only Molly could, she took his rebuke without showing signs of hurt. Only Benji could detect a small gesture that signaled her uneasiness. He had seen her brush back the stray curl that always seem to fall on her forehead many times when she had silently accepted harsh, undeserved words from his dad.

Pangs of guilt simply darkened his mood more, but it was beyond him to take back his words or to apologize. Molly's parting words echoed her usual kindness.

"Know how much I love you and that I will pray for both physical and emotional healing for you. I will be here whenever you decide you want me." Her sweet smile spoke more than did her words.

He could see no hope, but somehow, he felt a connection – a kinship – with this imposing figure looking down at him now. He had heard about him from some of the nurses. In trying to encourage Benji, they had told him some of this great surgeon's tenacity and courage and how he refused to give up.

How could this renowned surgeon have found a way to go on after losing an arm? How could he possibly do surgery with only one? His curiosity about this guy temporarily took his thoughts off his plight. Benji couldn't refrain from turning on his back to look at him once again.

"I'm not one of your doctors. I don't do orthopedics, but my friend, Dr. Skelton, your orthopedic surgeon, told me about your situation this morning and asked if I would drop by to see you. I'll be back in a few days to listen if you want to tell me about it. Here's my card. Feel free to call me if you need to talk. Both my office and cell numbers are on it."

Benji liked this athletically-built guy and had stared at his artificial limb hanging by his side, filling a void where his left arm would have been. "I would like to know your story too." Benji stammered half-heartedly, "Thanks for stopping by. Please come back soon." This was the most receptive he had been to anyone since his tragedy.

Reflections

It wasn't the incessant throbbing; it wasn't even the guilt that nagged him so often after he had been such a pain in the rear to everyone who tried to help him. This time the thoughts stealing his sleep were the words of the one-armed doctor. "You just can't undo some things," resonated throughout his being. The truth was he had lost one leg to the IED and the other one was really messed-up. Yes, his life was changed forever but tonight he realized he had a choice. He could let this totally destroy him – his faith, his dreams, his relationships – or he could just wrap his mind around the fact that it had happened and move on to make the best of things. He vacillated – part of him wanted to give up – to give in to the anger and pain, but glimpses of what life could be if he made the best of the situation entered his thought processes for the first time since that horrendous day in Afghanistan.

"You're not sleeping tonight?" asked Flo, the seasoned nurse who had remained unabashed by his snarly attitude. "Are you hurting, do you need more pain medication or a sleeping pill, or would you like for me to sit with you a while and talk?"

Benji managed a smile for her, one that hadn't surfaced since he had been at Walter Reed. "I'm okay. If I take more medicine, I won't be able to think straight, and that's what I'm trying to do tonight."

"Benji, that's a good thing; in fact, that is the most positive step you've taken. If you change your mind later and need something, buzz for me, okay?"

Temptation to take more sedation and to go back to the land of oblivion where he wouldn't have to try, where he wouldn't have to think about the future almost won. *I can go a little longer with the pain,* he thought. He reflected on the days when he would practice so hard for basketball and thought he would fall from exhaustion, but then he would do some self-talk and say, *I can go a little longer, I can try a bit harder, I can be a winner, if I don't give up.* His tenacity and determination had always been as big a factor in his sports success as was his innate talent.

A mental list of what he could do with the rest of his life was what he needed. *What do I love, what goals did I have before I went to Afghanistan, what can my handicapped-self do now? I loved basketball, but I guess a career as a pro is out of the question,* he sardonically chuckled. *When I was younger, I even thought about following my dad's footsteps into the ministry.* Then hostility

97

arose as bitter gall; *that really worked out well for him. I wonder if I would end up chasing skirts too. Besides, I'm not sure about God and that faith thing anymore.* For an hour or more, he mentally revisited the days when his dad Jack was found out, how his adulterous affair destroyed his ministry, how it almost destroyed the family. Then he remembered the days after his dad's life-changing automobile accident, and how his mom so selflessly cared for his every need. Almost, he went to the place in the past where God brought beauty from the ashes of this disaster, but anger stuck a foot in and wouldn't let him go there.

That was as far as he could go; nothing good was coming from his list-making. His resolve to keep trying disappeared. He buzzed the nurse to bring him his pain meds and a sleeping pill.

When sleep finally had its way with him, it wasn't restful. He was back in Afghanistan. There he stood by an old warehouse, one foot propped behind him against the building, and his weapon relaxed pointing downward in his arm. His buddy Cain assumed a similar position as the two rehashed the scenario from the previous night when Cain had taken all in their nightly poker game. "Mr. Luck camped out on your shoulder all night long. You just couldn't lose. Trevor thought he had that last game when you bluffed him out," laughed Benji.

"Luck has always been my middle name. You wouldn't believe how often I escaped one disaster or another by only a hair as I was growing up," replied the sandy-headed jovial guy. Just as the words left his lips, both soldiers flew into the air from the IED that exploded at their feet.

As Benji emerged from a daze, he looked to his right, close enough for him to reach out and touch what remained of lucky Cain. The pain and shock of what he saw numbed his realization of his own situation for only minutes. The pain, the shock of knowing his life would be changed forever, if he even survived, bounced back in his head. If only the blood-splattered ground would open up and consume him, it would be better than what he was facing. He reacted the only way his instincts allowed him to. He still could hear his own gut-wrenching screams and feel his life sinking into an awful abyss.

Flo shook him slightly and gently called his name. "Benji, Benji, wake up. You are having another nightmare. Everything is all right. You are safe."

Flo had an ethereal quality about her. She didn't have to be called; she just seemed to show up during the wee morning hours when he needed her most. She didn't seem

99

to have the social connection with the other nurses that most of the nurses did. Her bond was more with her patients. When she was on duty, she didn't spend most of her time sitting at the desk pushing papers and pretending to be busy, all the while gossiping about personal stuff, as did many of the nurses. He would often wake up and find her just standing over him. There was a hint of a memory of her during his first nights at Walter Reed, but he couldn't quite bring it to the surface; he just knew it was something really important.

His reflections on the possibilities of his future picked up where they left off earlier. *Was coaching a possibility? Did he want to go into some medical field where he might help others like that one-armed surgeon was doing?* Benji picked up the doctor's card that was still on the bedside table where he had left it. Dr. Jefferson Newell, M.D., said the card. *I just may give him a call and ask him to stop back by,* thought Benji.

An Epiphany

The next morning, Benji showed another sign of progress. When the day-shift R.N. made her early rounds, Benji told her, "You know, I think I will take you up on that offer you've been making. Being rolled out into the courtyard to get a few rays of sun would be nice if that's okay."

This thrilled his smiling nurse because she saw that attitude as progress. "That would not only be okay, but it would help you more than all this medicine. I can't say enough good things about sunlight therapy. If it doesn't help you physically, it certainly will mentally and emotionally."

He squinted as his eyes adjusted to the sunlight. It was a beautiful spring morning – a little nippy, but the sun shone brightly. With the heavy robe over his tacky hospital gown and wrapped snugly in a blanket, Benji found the cool temperature a refreshing change. He realized the hospital odors with which had become so familiar didn't exist outside. Benji almost started thanking God for the beautiful day, before he remembered he was mad at Him.

After a few minutes of solitude, he became aware of another patient sitting a few feet away. Not only was he sporting the same type leg bandages on a stump that Benji had, but this guy had bandages covering his eyes. "Is somebody else out here?" called the young soldier.

At first, Benji was tempted to stay silent and continue enjoying his privacy, but the second time the young man called out, Benji relented and answered, "I'm over here. Do you need something?"

"Not really, but I've developed this weird sense of just knowing when someone is near since I lost my eyesight. I'll leave you alone if you don't want to talk, but if you are interested, how about rolling over here where we can meet. I don't drive this thing too well without being able to see where I'm going. I've run over a few people already," he chuckled.

Not really wanting conversation, Benji was tempted to tell him he wasn't interested, but there was just something engaging about this redheaded, freckled-face guy with an infectious smile. Besides, Benji didn't have it in him to be rude to a fellow hurting soldier. Benji pushed the lever on his electric wheelchair and parked by him. "I'm Benji; who are you?"

"They call me Little Red but my name is really Phillip Snead. I'm from West Virginia. How about you? Where do you call home?"

"I'm from Georgia. How long have you been at Walter Reed?"

"I came in three months ago and will probably be here for many moons to come."

Their conversation consisted to a great extent of their injuries and the stories of what caused them. They had swapped family stories and broken dreams. Finally, Red, scratching his red head, got to more interesting matters. "Could I ask you something? I haven't breathed a word of this to anyone else here, but I just wanted to know if it was real or if I just dreamed it."

"Yeah, I guess we all do a lot of dreaming. Mine usually aren't very pleasant though."

Little Red faced him as though he could see his friend and responded as though what Benji said was the most unusual thing he had ever heard. "I know mine aren't either, except for that first night here, and I still don't know if it was a dream or not."

"You've piqued my interest for sure; go ahead."

"Do you know Flo, the night-shift nurse that just seems to appear out of nowhere?"

"Sure do. She has a special ability to be there when I need her most. I thought I was the only one that thought that a bit weird."

Red continued, "It took a while for the memory to clear up, but I think this really happened. One of my main concerns was neither losing my eyesight nor having a leg blown off, but I can remember wondering while I was still lying on the ground in a puddle of blood if my manhood was still intact."

Benji laughed. "That must be fairly common. I remember asking my buddies that very same thing while I was waiting for the gurney. We guys really have our priorities in order, don't we," he joked.

"Well, that brings me to the question. Did you receive – how can I say it - that special assurance from Flo?"

Benji sat silently for a few minutes trying to conjure up that mysterious thing about Flo he had been pondering. "I'm not sure. There's been something niggling me about her lately, but I just can't bring it into focus."

"I think she's a special angel; I finally recalled that first night when I was in a drugged stupor her crawling under the cover with me. Now don't get me wrong; it wasn't anything more, but she simply reassured me that things down there were in perfect working order if I ever again needed them."

It suddenly was like a light coming on – an epiphany. "That was it. I remember that happening, too," said Benji. His expression registered the surprise he felt at that memory "That's it. I finally recall what's so special about her, but since that night, I've never had a doubt about my equipment. Red, there was nothing dirty about what she did; it really was a ministry of sorts, but I think we need to keep this just between the two of us. To say the least, she wasn't following protocol, but I wouldn't do anything to get her in trouble."

The two soldiers sat enjoying a shared silence for a while. Then Red, at first, started humming; then he broke into song. "Bless the Lord, oh my soul, and all that is within me. Bless His holy name." It was more than a song though; it was a soul-stirring prayer of praise. Benji pondered the words and the sentiment of the one singing it. Shame and sorrow hit him like a bulldozer. If Red, who had far greater problems than he had, could sing praises to God, how thankless he had been for being as well off as he was. He had been mad at God for so long; now he only wanted to praise Him, too. In a soft, trembling voice, Benji joined in Red's song of praise. After a few moments, the two sang praise hymns so loudly the nurses gathered at the door just to listen.

Steps Forward

When Benji was back in his room, he picked up the phone and called Molly. "Mom, I've discovered you can't stay mad when you've been with Jesus."

"What, son? Are you worse? Have you had a near-death experience or something?" Anxiety filled her normally calm voice.

Benji laughed, "Nothing like that, Mom. I just called to say how sorry I am about the way I treated you when you were here. I'd love for you to come back for a visit when you get a chance. I met a friend – a fellow injured soldier – who was out on the porch. He started singing praise songs. Then I realized if he could praise Jesus in the shape he was in, I needed to put my sulking and self-pity aside and praise him too. That has done more for me than all the medicine in the world."

When Sydney, the therapist, came at his scheduled time, Benji greeted him. "Hi, buddy. What are you up to today?"

Sydney couldn't say a word for a minute. He just stood opened-mouth staring at his patient. "I must be in the wrong room. What have they done with Benji?" the therapist finally chuckled. Benji laughed at his reaction.

"Friend, I want you to work me hard; I'm ready to get some strength back and get in shape for my prosthesis."

"What is responsible for this positive change? Is this the same guy who has tried to run me off every time I've been in the room?"

"Nah, I sent that guy away. He was a real downer."

When Mrs. Fieldstone, Benji's least favorite nurse, came in later that day to administer his meds, Benji greeted her pleasantly. "Well, I guess you're finished with all that self-pity nonsense. You would have thought you were the only one who had ever been injured," she said.

"Well, when do you think you'll get that big 'ol grudge off your shoulder," Benji joked. "Anyway, what are you so unhappy about? You seem to have all your limbs intact, and it's evident you get plenty to eat." Although he did it all with a smile, he set Nurse Fieldstone down a notch.

"Hmm, that really wasn't necessary." She stomped out in a huff, leaving her med tray behind. In a few minutes, she returned.

"Forget something, sweetheart?" he teased.

The therapy, bandage changes, bath, and routine daily tedium had Benji worn-out, but not too tired to do as he had planned. He moved the things around on his bedside table until he found Dr. Newell's card again. *This is probably an effort in futility. I doubt that guy meant what he said about calling him if I ever wanted to talk. I know he must have more important things to do, but I'm going to give it a shot.* He dialed the office number listed and waited through five rings.

"Dr. Newell's office. May I help you?"

"This is Benji Pate over at Walter Reed. I wonder if I might talk to Dr. Newell."

"Could you tell me what the call is concerning?"

By that time, Benji was just too tired to go through doctors' office procedures. "Just forget it. He's probably too busy to talk anyway." Benji hung up a little discouraged. *I'll just take a nap before supper trays come.*

After supper and the night meds, Benji settled down reflecting on the day's blessings. He was in the stage between being awake and being totally asleep when he heard a knock at the door. "Come in."

In the dimness of the night light, Benji saw the outline of the tall one-armed doctor. "Hope I'm not too late, but this is as soon as I could come. I had surgeries all morning and an office full of patients this afternoon. The receptionist told me I had received a call from you."

"I'm surprised you actually came, and I feel guilty in taking your time after the day you've had. I guess I just wasn't ready to talk too much when you were here before. Could I ask you some questions, Dr. Newell?'

"I'm as open as a Case knife. You can ask me anything, but just call me Jeff, since I'm not here as your physician." Jeff pulled up a chair and sat near the bed.

"I've decided," Benji said with slow pauses, "to try to start some positive steps toward my recovery – not just physical, but emotional, as well. How did you do that?"

"Let's just say with a little help from my friend," he said wryly, indicating his prosthetic arm.

"I'm not unfamiliar with the different ways amputees face their losses. Some have periods of great remorse; some exhibit fear; some, not unlike you reject any comfort, consolation or advice for a while; but some recognize this as just another of life's hurdles they must jump. I guess I took the last attitude. I focused more on what I do have instead of what I've lost. I may have lost an arm, but I still have another one. I see it as mind over matter. Most amputees' biggest disability is between the ears – their attitude."

Jeff gave Benji a genuine smile and patted him on the shoulder. "Your acknowledging you're ready to move forward is your biggest step toward acceptance. You will find frustration in your limitation in doing some mundane things, but like me, you'll find a way to solve these issues eventually."

Benji silently nodded assent to what he was hearing. After taking time to absorb what Jeff had told him, "I've had to recount the circumstances surrounding losing my leg to the IED to Army personnel so many times, I sound like a broken record. Then any time someone new enters my room, they want to know details. I just get tired of talking about it."

"I wish I could tell you that you would be finished telling your story, but I can't. People will continue to ask – some out of concern – some out of nosiness. Just make up your mind that retelling it is therapy and it might help someone else in some way. Handle things the best way you can; even find some humor in some of the stuff."

"How could I ever find something to laugh at in this?" Benji said, pointing to where his leg should have been.

"Oh, I don't know. Situations will arise sooner or later that will seem somewhat comical. I met my brother the other day to go to the lake fishing. When we got well on our way, I started laughing. He asked what I was laughing about. I told him that I left my arm at home. Now how could anyone forget something so essential?"

Both young men enjoyed a belly laugh.

"How did you react when you discovered you had lost an arm? You must have been devastated, being a surgeon and all that? Did you go through great depression? How did you get back to where you are now?" The questions poured from Benji.

"You're tired and so am I. Can I come back and answer at least some of your questions another day? This conversation may last a while."

"Sure. I won't be going anywhere. You'll know where to find me."

"Listen, I'll be stopping back in soon. Call me if you need me before I get back."

Molly's Visit and News from Home

After therapy the next day, Benji decided to try some arm exercises on his own. He started lifting small weights and then progressed to attempting to do some modified pull-ups. It didn't take much for him to reach his boundaries. His energy level was still low.

After resting in his room a while and then having lunch, he decided to go back out to the courtyard hoping to find his friend Red. He enjoyed the sun and solitude a while before the nurse came out. "There you are. I thought you had escaped," she laughed. "I brought your meds and some water so you can stay out longer if you wish."

"I was hoping to find my friend who was here a few days ago."

"Who is he? I might be able to find him and see if he's up to coming out."

"Everybody calls him Red, but I believe he said his name is Phillip Snead or Reed or something like that. He had lost his sight."

The nurse's sudden change of expression told more than her words. "He is not on our unit, and sometimes it is hard to get info about patients on other floors."

"You don't lie well, you know. How about leveling with me. I can take it." If she didn't say the dreaded words, maybe it wasn't so, but Benji knew the truth, even before she spoke it.

"I'm so sorry; Benji, but he just couldn't make it. He had too many strikes against him. His latest bout with staph took its toll. He knew his days were numbered even when he was out here talking and singing with you."

I miss him already and really didn't know him that long. He was a light in a dark place. Benji took the edge of his blanket and brushed at the tears that had begun dripping onto his hands. *My dad used to preach that life was but a vapor, but that was before, before... I won't go there. It will just bring me down more.*

Nurse Vogel reappeared. Benji knew it wasn't time for more meds and she had said he could stay out longer. *What does she want?*

"Benji, you have a visitor. Would you like to come back in or do you want me to bring her out here?"

"Do you know who it is?"

"It's your mom."

Without even answering, Benji started his wheelchair back in. "Mom, I'm thrilled to see you. I didn't know you would be here today."

"I thought I would surprise you with a visit and with this." She drew from behind her back a box of Benji's favorites – her homemade chocolate chip cookies.

"Let me see. Which am I the happiest to see, you or the cookies," Benji teased as he opened his arms for his mom to enter an embrace that had been too long in coming.

This time it was Molly brushing away tears. "I've finally got my boy back – the real Benji."

"Sorry I've been such a pain, such a whiny baby."

"Don't apologize. You deserved to have your time of grief and if more comes, I'll understand that too. You may have thought you pushed me away, but there's no way you can escape your mom's care and prayers, young man."

Benji was an ever-flowing fountain of words. He rattled on and on with every detail, from the time he was injured, on to today when he learned his new friend died. Molly, nodding assent, expressing understanding and occasionally uttering a "yes," absorbed each syllable with rapt attention. As his saga slowed and finally came to an end, Molly gave him a bear hug.

"I love you as my son more than you will ever know, and now I claim you as my hero."

Looking intently into his mother's eyes, Benji said, "Mom, I knew you were with me each step of the way even though I didn't acknowledge it to you. Although I haven't been on good terms with God lately, the words from Romans, chapter 8, I believe, resonated in my soul - *For I am persuaded, that neither death, nor life, nor angels, nor principalities, nor powers, nor things present, nor things to come, Nor height, nor depth, nor any other creature, shall be able to separate us from the love of God, which is in Christ Jesus our Lord.* I knew that nothing, not even my snarly attitude, could separate me from your love either."

"Now tell me about everybody at home."

"Thad is great and staying busy doing volunteer work. We are even planning to go with a group from church on a medical mission to Dominican Republic in a few months. Caitlin and Bob are better than ever and staying busy with all of Emily's activities. Celeste comes at least twice a month and hasn't ceased praying for you. She has a new love interest we've met, and he has received the family's stamp of approval. They are all eager to come see you when you give the go-ahead. Caitlin has news she

115

wants to tell you herself. Benji, you can't believe the support you have at home from friends and church family. We get calls daily asking of your welfare." Molly paused and took on an unsure countenance. She adjusted her position and leaned toward Benji. "There is one especially who asks daily if we have updates, but I don't know if you are ready to hear about her."

"Who is it, Mom? Reach over to that basket on the floor and take out the top unopened letter. Could it be from her?"

Molly found the mountain of cards and letters and immediately saw the top one had Belinda Sandlin's name on the return address. "You haven't opened it?"

"I haven't been in the right frame of mind to deal with her sympathy"

"I understand, but I sense her feelings for you go beyond sympathy. When you feel ready, she wants to see you face-to-face to tell you how sorry she is for breaking up with you, but that can come only if, and when, you want to see her. Everyone understands they can't overwhelm you all at once."

Trying to make this visit a positive one, she didn't mention his high school buds, for she didn't want it to lead to the discussion about PeeWee and his bout with drug addiction. She certainly didn't want to disclose the terrible experience she had had when he broke in their house.

"I'm getting better, Mom, especially after unloading on you today, but I think I'd rather see the others on home ground. The doctors are discussing a possible furlough for me from here for a week or two. I'd like to see them all then. Give me some time to read what Belinda has to say, and I'll think on what I want to do there."

The Epistles

After his mom left, Benji sat in his wheelchair in the courtyard until dark, musing over their conversation. He had such mixed emotions about returning home for a furlough. He wanted to reunite with family so very much, but at the same time, didn't know how he could handle sympathetic looks or words. He appreciated the prayers and concerns and really wanted to express his gratitude to everyone, but at the same time, he knew the relationships he had had before would now always be filtered through thoughts of his injuries and of the physical changes in him. He wished so desperately that everything would be the same as it was the day he left. Finally he told himself, "That is a bunch of self-pitying nonsense. Shake it off, Benji, and get on with life." A slight grin came over his face as he realized how much his self-talk was colored by his conversations with Dr. Newell.

But then a fear and uneasiness gripped him as he thought of tackling the stack of letters from Belinda. He kneaded the space between his eyes with his fingers, as he only did when he was perplexed. Was it that or was it the chill from the cool, sunless air? Nonetheless, he knew he needed to roll back in. As he did, he realized how much he missed his new-found friend Red. He had a sense he could have talked with him about this and used him as a sounding board.

After nibbling at his tasteless chicken casserole and green beans, he pushed aside his tray and reached for the letters. *Where should I start, the first ones or the most recent?* He opted for the last letter she had written.

Dear Benji,

Today has been little different from the ones from past weeks. My life has fallen into such a routine; I feel I operate on autopilot. Get up, go the Dr. Jones' office for my day's work, deal with all the tedium involved in setting up instrument trays for the doctor's countless oral surgery cases, talk to anxious family members and reassure them the patient was doing great. On and on it goes. The only true bright spot in my day is when I go by daycare and pick up sweet Beau. I never knew what joy a baby could bring to my life.

Benji dropped the letter in disbelief. *Who in the name of --- is Beau? Maybe I should have started at the first of the stack, but I'm afraid to. Has Belinda married? No, that couldn't be, because she still has her maiden name. It can't be mine; we never had real sex, just some heavy petting.*

Then anger took over as Benji faced the fact she had been sleeping around. Why was she continuing writing him? He threw the stack of the letters in the floor, with the intention of never picking them back up.

The staff noticed a change in Benji's attitude and recognized depression was creeping in again. The nurses reported this to Dr. Skelton. "Morning Benji," he said as he started his routine evaluation of him. "Any problems, pain or anything unusual you need to tell me about?"

"No, things are about like they've been." Benji's dark countenance told more than did his words.

"How about being straight with me. We have too much between us to play games. I can see it in your eyes; something is bothering you. If it isn't physical, it's something more. Do you need me to send in the psychiatrist or chaplain so you can talk it out? You have been doing so much better emotionally lately. I don't want a relapse."

"No, I'd rather you didn't. Some things need not be aired."

"Have it your way today, but if I don't see you bouncing back pretty soon, I'll have no choice."

Benji resolved to put on a happier face for the staff. He wasn't ready to talk about his problems right then. Maybe he needed to go back to the beginning of the letters to try to sort this out. He needed to hear what Belinda had to say even though he doubted she would be truthful. Benji started scanning the letters one-by-one. Mostly the first ones were a mixture of Belinda saying she was concerned about him and that she was praying for him daily. She would share what little news from home she could think of. On into the stack, one letter got his attention: *Benji, I really miss you and the relationship we had, but you aren't answering my letters. I know you are receiving them because your mother has indicated you are answering hers whenever you can. I'm really lonely and wondered what you would think of my dating some. One of our patients is a guy who was in college with us. He has asked me out several times. I feel awkward even thinking about dating anyone else, but I gather you had just as soon forget me.*

Benji dropped the letter on the bed, angry at the thought of Belinda being with someone else. But what should he expect? Did he think she would cloister herself forever even though they weren't an item anymore?

It was the next morning before he even considered picking the letters back up. He would quickly scan each letter wondering how long it would be before she would give

121

up on writing these meaningless mails. They were postmarked about three days apart. Therefore, the news changed little, although she would drop in a tidbit now and then about going somewhere with Dirk – to the movies, a dance, a picnic, a concert and so on. She said very little though about their relationship. He only wondered how serious it might be.

In one letter she did imply that he was more demanding than she liked. "He wants to go into territory I'm not ready for. I enjoy having someone to go places with, but I intend to save sex for marriage. I may have to break this off."

Benji noticed the date. When he picked up the next letter, he realized a significant gap in the dates. *I probably just got them out of line*, Benji told himself. He thought little more about it until he started reading the next one. It was short and different from the rest: *Benji, I wish you were here. There are some things I really would like to tell you about, but I can't do it in the letter. I don't need to burden you with my problems if you are even reading this.*

That one got Benji's attention. *What was it she couldn't write? I hope it's not the details of her tryst with Dirk,* he thought.

In several of the following letters, Belinda spoke of not feeling well. In one, she said she was taking some time off work for a while. "I hate to be a burden on my parents, but I guess I will have to move back in with them for a while."

Was this mystery stuff just a ploy to get him to write back, or was Belinda sick? Benji decided he would call his mom the next day and try to get some input from her without saying too much about the letters.

Molly wasn't very forthcoming with information when Benji tried to draw her into conversation about Belinda. "Mom, I'm trying to sort out what I want and what I don't when it comes to seeing Belinda. What can you tell me about her? I haven't talked with her since I left. What's she doing? Is she dating? How about her health?"

"All I will say is Belinda has had a really tough time in many ways since you left. As far as details go, I really think those are hers to share. I think you should consider letting her come up to tell you some things, face-to-face. She really cares about you, but what you do about that is totally yours to decide after you hear her out."

After his conversation with Molly, Benji was baffled. *Did he want to know more than he had surmised already? Was Belinda sick? Who was the father of her son?*

Benji picked up the monumental stack of letters and tired at the thought of plowing through all of them. He just laid them back down. *What could it hurt to just hear Belinda out? I guess I really do care about her, or I wouldn't have read this far. BUT has she been sleeping around? I know I could have gone farther with her if I'd tried. Is it worth it to even listen?* Benji's feelings toward Belinda were going back and forth like an oscillating fan.

From Somewhere Deep Within

That night just as Benji was drifting off, a tap came at the door. "Am I too late to see my friend tonight," Dr. Newell said with that perpetual grin.

"No, please come in. I doubt that I will get very restful sleep tonight anyway."

With his smile turning to a concerned frown, Dr. Newell asked, "You're not fighting another infection, are you?"

"No. I don't think penicillin will take care of this ailment," Benji replied with a less than sincere smile.

The lanky doctor pulled up a straight chair, turned it backward, straddled it facing Benji, and resting his chin on the chair back, he replied, "I'm listening, pal."

Benji told him about the letters and about his quandary. "I don't know whether to let her come and tell me what's going on, or if I even care."

Suddenly Dr. Newell's demeanor changed. "Drop her like a hot potato, Benji. It's evident she's been whoring around. You need her about like you need to step on another IED. She's no good and doesn't deserve you or your sacrifice." Benji had never seen this bitter side of his friend, nor did he like it, nor did he appreciate his

125

assessment of Belinda. He didn't even know her.

Benji bristled. "Where do you come off saying stuff like this about her? You don't know her. I don't know what has gone on, but at least she deserves to be heard out."

That gentle, mild-manner returned, and Dr. Newell smirked, "Well, there you have it. Your dilemma is solved. Call her tomorrow and hear her out." He put the turned chair back around, and bade Benji a good night.

Still shocked by the psychological ploy his friend had used, Benji shook his head and wondered where that defensiveness had come from. He knew it was from some place deep within him. He slept more deeply that night than he had in days. In his dreams, he saw Belinda dressed in a white flowing gown bidding him to come join her in the clouds.

Things Aren't Always As They Appear

The next day Benji spent most of the day trying to call Belinda. If he was going to do this, he knew he had to do it before he backed out. No answer. "Please leave a message after the beep." He heard this recorded message time after time from both her home and cell numbers. Doubts and bitterness began to creep in. Was this the Lord's way of telling him to leave it alone? Was she too busy out gallivanting to even answer her phone? Or maybe she saw his number on the caller ID and didn't want to talk to him.

More confused than ever, that night he picked up his bible and began reading. He couldn't keep his mind on what he was trying to read for long, but one verse kept niggling him - *And we know that all things work together for good to them that love God, to them who are the called according to his purpose.* Romans 8:28

Hmph! That's not working out so well for me right now, Lord. I know you said you wouldn't put more on us than we could bear, but sometimes I need you to pick up the heavy end of the board and help me out. I try to pray to you, but you seem so distant. I really need some help; I can handle the physical stuff better than I can cope with the stress of just not knowing – not knowing what I should or shouldn't do where Belinda is concerned. If I could just have some reassurance that you are with me each step of the way...

He must have fallen asleep talking to the Father because he suddenly roused with the sense that someone was in the room with him. Sure enough towering over his bed was his one-armed pal. "What is it with you, guy? I don't see you for weeks and suddenly you show up two nights in a row."

"I just wanted to hear about the next chapter in your saga. Did you make the call today?"

"I tried but never got through. But on another matter, you really got me yesterday." Benji did his lopped-sided grin. "I thought I had met the real Mr. Hyde. I've never seen anyone transform from an easygoing dude, to such a bitter, nasty creature. You must have learned that tactic in Medical Psychology 101 or something." They both laughed.

Jeff Newell stood awkwardly silent with his head hanging for several long minutes. "Listen, Benji. That wasn't completely for show. I guess it was a classic case of transference. I shouldn't share my trash with you, but since we've gone this far, I guess I should level with you. When you told me about Belinda and the baby, the situation with my wife came to the forefront. Susan, my wife for some thirty years, is the one that's gone 'a-whoring.' I found her in my bed with my best friend a while back. I surprised her one night by coming home early. She had begun to be disinterested in me and what was going on with my career; she didn't even care about the awards I had received. You have some idea of the long hours I keep. I had begun to get a sense that she was growing weary of the years of eating dinner alone or with the children when they were still living at home. I decided one night to surprise her and knock off early. A night out together might heal some wounds. I guess I was the one who got the surprise. At the time, I couldn't react with anger or violence toward him nor her. I was cut to the quick deep in my soul to see the one who had promised 'to love and honor 'til death do us part' cavorting with the one who had stood by me through thick and thin, the one who had been my best man in our wedding. The anger and bitterness came later and has stayed with me for three years now. I haven't even talked to her since that night. She has called and left messages, expressing sorrow and regret, but those words mean absolutely nothing. I'm through with that trashy woman. I hope to never see her again. I guess, for a moment last night, all that came pouring in my mind, and for that moment, I really meant what I said."

Now, it was Benji's turn. "Okay, big boy." Benji realized that wasn't a very respectful way to address Dr. Newell, but it just came out. Then he continued, "It's your time to sit down and listen to me. You get your "feel goods" and fulfillment in your career. You help a lot of people and receive praise and accolades for it. You have achieved much and deserve praise. But how much time have you spent thinking about the fact your wife doesn't have that; she doesn't even get to be a part of that life. All she has gotten for years is what is left over of you at the end of stressful days. I'm not saying what she did was right or excusable, but I am saying you might give some thought to your part in the adultery. Maybe your career has been your mistress. I don't know. I don't know that much about you, but what I do know is that we are all sinners. The sin may be different from one person to the next, but we're all flawed. All I'm saying is that if she was worth marrying, birthing your children, and probably staying faithful for years, don't you think she's worth hearing out? I'm giving you an assignment. Go home. Sit down and reflect on the girl you married. You might consider taking a new look at your wedding pictures. What good did you see in her then? How much of that is still there? Did you mean your vows – for better or worse – 'til death do us part?"

"Then start naming your own sins one-by-one – the sins of commission and of omission. The scriptures tell us that ALL have sinned and come short of the glory of God, but if we confess our sins to Him, he is willing to forgive them. First, you may need to sort out your relationship with the one who created you, the one who suffered and died on the cross for YOUR sins. How much praise have you given him?"

Jeff sat stunned for minutes before he could speak. "Where in the --- did that come from? Are you a preacher or something? Where do you come off lecturing to ME anyway? All I've ever done was to try to befriend you."

Jeff stood with his eyes ablaze with anger. Pointing his finger at Benji, he shouted, "Don't you ever talk to me that way again, you little do-gooder, bible thumper." He stomped out and slammed the door closed.

Now, God, that didn't go very well, did it? I don't know where that sermonette came from, nor do I know where I found the guts to talk to my friend that way. I ask your forgiveness for doing it wrong so often. I'm not worthy to even share your words with others when half the time I'm filled with hate and bitterness myself.

The Call

Benji was startled when the phone rang at 10 p.m. He hesitated before he answered. Maybe Jeff Newell wasn't through berating him; he just didn't want to hear anymore. But the ringing continued, and it wasn't in Benji's curious nature not to answer.

The voice on the other end was soft and shaky. Timidly, Belinda said, "Benji, I see where you have been trying to call me. It's taken a while for me to muster the courage to return your calls."

"It's really good to hear your voice again, Belinda. I thought maybe you had written me off completely. I was calling you to ask a favor. I was wondering if you could find the time to come up to Walter Reed to see me if I sent you a plane ticket. I think we must have a lot of catching up to do, and I wanted to talk with you privately before I came home on furlough."

There was what seemed to be an interminable pause before she answered. "Are you really sure you want that? I don't know how much you know, if you have read my letters or if news about me has reached you. I know you've been through so much."

"I confess. I haven't read many of your letters, but I started scanning a few days

133

ago. I decided I had rather hear everything from you than wading through the unread letters."

"Benji, it's not a pretty story. I've begun trying to put my life back on track, but I'm not sure I'm ready for your disapproval. I know you will be disappointed in me, but if you really want me to, I guess I could come this weekend. I'll have to see if your mom will keep Beau."

"I'll make you a deal. If you won't come with pity for me in your eyes, I'll hold my judgment until I hear you out. Belinda. I still care about you."

Belinda's Visit

Benji didn't have to wait long for his answer. The next morning, Belinda called before she went to work to say Molly would care for Beau and she could come on Saturday if that was okay. Benji quickly assured her the airline ticket would be in her inbox as soon as she got home that afternoon. Benji was as excited as a five-year-old anticipating a birthday. The many unanswered questions made him nervous, but that didn't overshadow his anticipation. When doubts about what had happened arose, thoughts of that impromptu sermon he had given to Jeff Newell reminded him that if she had sinned, who was he to condemn her? He was just a sinner saved by grace.

When the nurse came in to see if he would like to go to the courtyard to sit in the sun for a while, he surprised her by answering, "I'm too busy today."

"What could he be so busy doing?" she pondered.

"Could you get the number for Delta reservations for me? I can't seem to find it using my cell. The signal in here is just off and on."

"Sure. Are you flying the coop or something? Your furlough is still pending, you know."

"No, it's not for me but for a friend who's coming in Saturday. Will you be working then? I'd like you to meet her."

"I'm scheduled for Saturday, but if I weren't, I'd switch with someone because you have intrigued me. I'm looking forward to meeting this person that has put such a glow in your eyes."

Saturday morning, Benji asked the orderly to get out some of his civilian duds for him to put on after his bath. Tailless hospital gowns had been his uniform for many weeks, but he thought he would look healthier and more complete – more normal in civvies.

Similar thoughts about looking good had occurred to Belinda also. She put on a nice pants outfit and applied her make-up with great care. She used concealer to cover the dark circles under her eyes. Although this ensemble was baggy on her, as were all of her clothes, it fit better than most. Looking in the mirror she assessed her image and determined she had done the best she could with what she had to work with. She had slept little the night before dreading telling Benji all that had happened. *How can he ever forgive me or see me in a positive light again? I can't forgive myself. But I guess it's time to face the music.*

The flight from Atlanta to Ronald Reagan Airport was quick and uneventful. Per Benji's instructions, Belinda took a taxi to the hospital. She had his room number written on her scratch pad though she didn't need to even look at it. She had repeated it over and over during the flight – Bldg. 10, Eagle Bldg., 4th floor, Room 411. When she tapped at the door, Benji immediately invited her in. Belinda entered and stood silent for a moment. Finally, she got her words back and greeted Benji. "Hi there," she said reticently, unsure of how she would be received.

Benji held out his arms for her from his wheel chair. "Don't 'Hi there' me, girl. Come and give me a hug." The ice was broken. He told Belinda she could either pull up a chair or sit on his bed. She opted for the bed because it was nearer to him. After they dispensed with the niceties - the 'how-are-yous' and such, Belinda began. While she had her courage she thought it best to get her story out. "Benji, you may want me to leave before I get too far into this. I will respect it if you do. I'm so sorry for all that's happened. I don't know how much you know from my letters, but you indicated you hadn't read many of them. I'll just start where we left off. After I broke off our relationship,

137

there hasn't been a day that I haven't regretted it. You were already such an integral part of my life, I felt totally incomplete without you. Seemingly, all your buddies, your friends and mine, still saw us as a couple and were very loyal to you. I was marked as "Benji's girl." Therefore, the calls for dates didn't come."

A muscle in Benji's jaw twitched at what she said. *Was she planning to fall into the arms of one of my friends as soon as I was out of the picture? If so, that little plan failed.* A chip in his determination to withhold judgment must have let those thoughts come through.

"I fell into the routine of getting up, going to work, coming home to do the chores I felt like doing, and watching some TV. Before going to bed, I would call your mom to see if she had any news from you. Occasionally, I would go to a movie with some of my girlfriends. As you can see from that stack of letters, I often found time to drop you a line in hopes that someday I would get a response. That never happened, but I don't mean that it a disparaging way," she quickly added. "I understand you wanted nothing more to do with me."

Benji was saddened to see his lovely Belinda so pale, so downtrodden and thin.

"I was still young and longed for male attention and contact. With Smytheville being small and a close community, the dates just weren't happening. One day, we got a new patient. You may remember him from college – Dirk Mason. I think we had a few classes with him. He came in, looking like he had just walked out of GQ. He appeared to be very successful in his real estate career. He showed an interest in me and was full of compliments that I know now were just his playboy lines. When he asked me out, I didn't hesitate to accept.

As I told you in one of the letters, he pressed me for more than I was willing to give. With a smokescreen of humor, he made comments about my being Mother Teresa. Then the jabs got a little more direct. 'Don't you know that girls your age are no longer virgins? You need to get in the real world, dear. You are the only person I know who believes they'll go to hell if they don't go to church every time the doors open.' He asked me if I really thought the man upstairs cared if I had sex or not. He laughed at my beliefs.

I tried to defend my faith and lifestyle, but was inadequate to verbally compete with him. He seemed so worldly and knowledgeable about everything. I was attracted to him although he made me uncomfortable. I made the mistake of continuing dating him. After we had gone out for dinner one night, he asked me to come to his apartment to watch a movie. An inner voice told me that wasn't such a good idea, but he was so convincing that it was just a movie. 'Surely you aren't such a prude, you can't even come up and watch a flick with me,' he chided.

Come in here to my computer before we turn on the movie; there's something I want you to see. I want you to see how real women act. You are so naïve, you have no clue how the rest of the world acts.

When he turned the screen on, there were couples doing things I could never have imagined. I tried not to watch, but for a few minutes I was mesmerized. Then he started coming on heavy. I said. 'Dirk, I don't want to do this. You said we were going to just watch a movie.'

After a few snide remarks, he said, 'Okay, okay, but, young lady, you won't be able to keep that Victorian guard up forever.'

The movie turned out to be little better than the porn on his computer, but I said nothing. He snuggled me close and before long, his hands started going to territories that had been off limits before. I tried to brush them away in the beginning, but I wasn't forceful enough."

By this time, tears of guilt were pouring down Belinda's face, and her saga was interrupted with sobs. Benji, in spite of the anger boiling up, reached over and patted her hand to comfort her.

"Before I knew what was happening, he was on top of me, undressing both of us. I kept saying, 'No, No!' but I guess part of me wasn't resisting enough. Benji, I know it was my fault and I'm so sorry."

By that time, Benji's face was scarlet with fury, not at Belinda, but at this scum bag who had taken advantage of her. His sense of protectiveness reminded him how much he still cared for her.

"You told him no repeatedly?"

"Yes, but it's my fault I know because I didn't resist strongly enough."

"Belinda, 'NO' is a complete sentence. It doesn't require justification or explanation. NO is NO and every guy worth his salt knows that. Dirk the jerk took advantage of you and your innocence."

At that, Belinda completely lost control, dropped her head on the bed, and wept uncontrollably.

Benji held her face up. "I just have one question? Was that the only time or have there been others since."

"No, he was the only one and that was the only time. I didn't ever want to be with anyone after that."

"I ran out of his apartment that night, not waiting for him to drive me home. I ran and walked the entire three miles to my place. I never answered his calls again, and he never came over. I did receive many obscene calls from his buddies. I only picked up on the first one, but after that, they left lurid messages on my voice mail making indecent proposals. They thought I was available to anyone anytime from what Dirk had told them. I guess by putting me down, it made him feel better about what he had done. He was also building his defense, painting me as one who slept around just in case I yelled rape to the police, but I wasn't going to do that; I wasn't going to put myself through that humiliation."

Benji, took her in his arms rocking her like a baby. "It's okay; everything's okay, baby. It's not your fault," he said soothing her with touch and words.

Both were broken; Benji, physically and Belinda, emotionally, but somehow it didn't matter at that moment. They both felt whole as they clung to each other as though they completed each other.

More Of The Story

The next morning Belinda returned to Benji's room refreshed and happier than she had been in months. A good night's sleep in the room Benji had pre-arranged for her and the burden of guilt somewhat lifted off her shoulders made her glow with a youthful countenance she had thought was lost forever. Now she was ready to hear out what Benji had to say. He had promised to share details of what had gone on with him and the journey of his thoughts throughout their separation.

The nursing staff had some idea about this important meeting, so they took care of helping him in the shower and giving the morning meds before she arrived. When she entered the room, Benji couldn't believe the transformation before him. Only then did he realize how haggard she was when she first arrived.

"Belinda, I had somehow forgotten just how beautiful you are. You are simply radiant today."

"You don't look so shabby yourself, Benji. My heart jumped up in my throat when I saw you again yesterday. I have to confess, you've always had that effect on me."

Belinda went to where he sat in a wheelchair and gave him a loving embrace, which he responded to with a kiss. "I did a lot of talking yesterday. Now tell me all about what has transpired in your life."

"What do you want to hear first – about my injuries and surgeries or about my thought process?"

"I know all you have communicated to your mom about the physical; I'd like to know where, or if, I've been in your thoughts."

"I can truthfully say, not a day has passed that I haven't thought about you. To be truthful, most of my contemplations were filled with bitterness and regret. Although I understood your breaking off our relationship because you were tired of waiting, I'll confess, I was also angry. You can't have those feelings about anyone you don't care about strongly. I wouldn't let mom tell me anything concerning you, although she tried. It made me irritated every time I got a letter from you, so I tossed it aside. You notice though, I didn't throw them away. I guess that shows I hadn't completely given up on you – and us.

"I've imagined your having a great time with friends and with other guys. That part was just about more than I could take. I didn't realize what a difficult time you were having. Other than my thoughts about you, I have gone the gamut with my emotions. I think I have hit every step of the grief process. Anger and depression just about took over. I felt dead, even though I was breathing. I really thought my life was over, at least the part that saw any bright spot in the future. It took a good friend – a one-armed doctor – to bring me out of my pit of pity, but I think I've run him off now, but that's another story."

Benji dropped his head and tears formed in his eyes. "Belinda, I'm sorry to tell you I'm not exactly pure anymore. I also broke my vow of staying chaste until marriage, and I wasn't raped. Before we shipped out, the other guys and I had a few wild nights on the town. There were prostitutes involved. I had no feelings for them, but nonetheless, it took me to a place from which I can never return. Once you lose your virginity, whether you enjoy the experience or not, you can't go back. You just can't undo some things."

It was almost time for lunch before Benji finished his saga. "But, Belinda, you still haven't told me what's gone on since that night."

"It doesn't get a lot better for a while. I didn't feel like I could tell anyone what had happened. I couldn't go to the police and cry rape because I felt responsible. The sickness began soon after I missed my first period. It was so bad and so constant; morning sickness can't come close to describing it. I was sick all day. I missed many days of work. I didn't know what to do, but I saw I couldn't keep up my rent if I couldn't work. I called Dirk, not because I wanted anymore to do with him, but because I thought he should know. I hoped he would at least take financial responsibility. I hadn't heard from him since I ran off that night. When I told him I was pretty sure I was pregnant, he brushed me off, big time.

He sneered and shouted, 'Why are you telling me this? Belinda, we barely had a one night fling. I guess you weren't the goody-two-shoes I thought you were. Maybe you better call some of the others you've been with. I don't believe the baby is mine, so, as far as I'm concerned, you can get rid of it. I really don't care about you or the baby. Leave me out of your drama. I want no part of fatherhood. And, by the way, if you choose to pursue this with the law, I have a line-up of buddies that will swear in court they've been with you.'

Benji, I didn't know what to do. I knew abortion was murder and that wasn't an option. After I finally lost my job because I had called in sick so often, I went to my parents. Benji, they have never been the warm, loving people like your mom and Thad, but I never believed they would react like they did. The night I went home, for, what I thought was to stay, my dad said things, unbelievable demeaning things.

'You got yourself into this mess sleeping around; now take care of your own problems. We don't want you bringing your disgrace in on us.' Those were just some of the insults he threw at me. Mom was no better. Although she didn't say that much, she just clung to him and nodded in agreement.

I left totally dejected, rejected, and sick. I didn't know where I was going; I just started walking down street after street. Finally, I guess I collapsed, because when I awoke, I was in the hospital. Thad was standing there. He asked, 'Belinda, are you feeling better now? When you were brought into the ER last night, one of the nurses knew you from church. She called your parents, but they said, in essence, they had broken-off relations with you. She, in turn, called me to see what she should do. She knew you and Benji were once engaged. So that's why I'm here. I came to see what I could do.'

"I told him I couldn't believe he would have come."

'You know Molly and I still care for you, regardless of what happened between you and Benji,' he told me. 'You came in dehydrated. When the ER doctor finished the examination, he discovered you are pregnant.'

I had never felt such shame in all my life. I couldn't look Dr. Thad in the eyes.

After I told him an abbreviated account of all that had transpired and about how I was too sick to work, he said, 'You are coming home with me when they release you, after you finish these intravenous fluids. I've already called Molly; she insists you stay with us for the time being.'

Benji, they are the kindest people I've ever known. I'm still with them. They took care of me the entire dreadful six months after my collapse. Even though they know the baby isn't yours, they love Beau like he's blood. I've got my job back now, but they insist I stay with them until I get more financially stable."

When one of his favorite nurses brought in his midday meds, he introduced Belinda. "This is the visitor I told you I wanted you to meet." He looked at Belinda with that smile and twinkle that so endeared him to everyone and told the nurse, "This is my fiancée," then paused, looking at Belinda for her reaction, "I think." He raised his eyebrows as though that was question. "I guess that's an original proposal." All three had a pleasant chuckle. Total elation filled the room.

New Leg And Homeward Bound

Decisions were made by Benji's medical team that it would be better for him to wait until he was walking on a new leg before giving him a furlough for his first trip home. That suited Benji. He wanted to be as whole as possible before friends and family saw him. He didn't accept pity well.

Shortly after his amputation, a pressure sock was placed on his stump to reduce the swelling and to prepare it for his prosthesis. One day a new face appeared in Benji's room. "Hi there. My name is Joyce Cooper. I'm a certified prosthetist who will be working with you and fitting you with your new friend – your leg."

Benji grinned and remarked, "I guess you've heard the old country song about a boy named Sue, haven't you? I was a bit taken back when you said your name was Joyce."

"Yeah, I've heard it all. I guess that helped me develop this tough hide, so now when people call me Crip or Peg Leg, I don't flinch too much," Joyce joshed as he lifted his pants leg revealing his own prosthesis.

"We'll be a team as I help you adjust to your artificial leg. I am well familiar with the physical, emotional, and even spiritual toll it will be. You think you've already been through much of that, but this is a new page in that book."

Joyce led on with many questions about Benji's expectations, his general health, his projected physical activity and many more questions.

"I don't mind, but why all this interrogation?'

"Believe it or not, your answers are all indication of your adjustment or lack thereof. It also helps in our choosing the best prosthesis option for you. These things can be very personalized. In fact, improvements are being made every year. We are trying to make them where you hardly realize the difference in the prosthesis and the leg you were born with. I have to admit, we are far from that today, but there have been so many improvements made since I got my first one ten years ago. Also, it will be imperative that you are real with me. Don't try to be more heroic than you already are; tell me when you have any pain, or even discomfort with it at all because that is the only way we can make adjustments with pressure spots that you will get in the beginning. We have a new design with flexible interfacing that provides more comfort and control than did the older models. We will take measurements today and something like a computer impression. I will then take that with me and the design process will begin."

"I find the prospect of being able to get around without crutches totally unreal, I have to tell you, friend." And that's exactly how Benji already thought of Mr. Joyce Cooper, CP. There was an inner connection. Benji didn't know exactly why yet, but he knew he would ask questions at their next encounter.

Joyce answered Benji. "I know that feeling, but believe it or not, all your emotions may not be positive. When I first got mine, I had such bouts of frustration with pressure sores, it not working like my real leg, having to come out of it for long periods to allow sores to heal – I could go on, but I don't want to steal your joy for the moment. I got so upset at one point, I told my wife to take it and throw it away. I think she wanted to toss me out instead, but that's another story for another day. Besides, many of the problems I had are greatly reduced with the new prosthesis developments. I'll be back in a couple of days. My talk therapy is as important as my teaching you about the mechanics of the leg."

The day he received his new leg was an emotional one. "It will take some getting used to and some therapy for you to be proficient with it," commented his therapist.

"We will work you hard so you can make that trip home as soon as possible."

It didn't take long for Benji to adjust to his prosthesis. He challenged it with great determination. Often the therapist would call a halt to the therapy session. "Benji, we don't want you to wear it out the first week. If you go at it too hard, too soon, you will make your stump so tender you will have to keep it off a while."

Finally, the order came down that Benji would have a two-week furlough. He quickly called Molly. "You think you could drive up here and drive an old crippled guy back home?"

For a few seconds, Molly was unable to respond. Many times she felt that day would never come. Tears rolled down her cheeks as she looked up and quietly said, "Praise you, Jesus." Then with a shaky voice that exposed her emotions, she whispered, "Yes, yes, yes." As she got better control, she cleared her voice and said, "Just tell me the day and time. We'll be there."

After they discussed pertinent details, Benji asked, "Would you do one more thing? If there's room, I'd like you to bring Belinda and Beau."

"No problem. We will come in the Navigator and there will be plenty of room. You can have a seat to yourself to stretch out if you need to. I'll bring a pile of pillows and a throw."

Benji often picked up on the slightest things to praise God for. When Molly casually mentioned picking him up in the Navigator, he remembered his mom always getting the oldest, most beat up car in the family. Of course she didn't have an image to maintain, was his Dad's reasoning, and he felt he did. He always managed the latest and best model for himself. No one else in the family seemed worthy to ride in it, much less drive it. Thad was so different. He insisted on Molly having the best of everything, even when she protested she didn't need finery. "Thank you, Lord, for bringing my mom such a blessing."

Two days later, Benji was made comfortable and was headed home. Just before they drove away, a nurse appeared at Benji's window. "You aren't leaving without my bidding you a sweet farewell, friend," spoke this angel dressed as a nurse.

"Oh, Flo, I want you to meet my family." Benji made the introductions and told them, "All the nurses have been wonderful, well, most anyway, but this one will always hold a special place in my heart." Then to Flo, "I would have hunted you down if this was permanent, but I'll be back. I'm just on furlough for a couple of weeks."

With a faraway stare, Flo replied, "I know, but we never know when a goodbye will be our last."

Benji was too excited about his own situation to read too much into her comment at the time. Rather than opting to lie down, he said, "I want Belinda and Beau on the seat with me." From the first time he had laid eyes on the nine-month-old, the child had captured his heart. "I don't believe I could love him more if he were my own flesh and blood. But if it is okay with you Belinda, from this day forward, he is my own," Benji told her when he first held Beau.

The vehicle was echoing with conversation - questions, explanations, praises – most of the time, several were talking at once. Finally, Benji's tranquilizers and mild pain meds kicked in, and he started drifting off.

Belinda gently nudged him when they reached a town sixty miles out of Smytheville. She ran her hand through his tousled hair in order to smooth it down. "I thought you would want to see this." The highway was filled with people and vehicles – some standing by the highway with placards, some inside cars, blowing the horns. Messages of varying kinds were held high - *Welcome home, Benji, You are my hero, Thanks for your service, we love you, and our prayers have been with you.* Everyone in the car became overwhelmed when they passed a group of veterans, all missing limbs, with a sign that said, *We are with you in your recovery.* The Atlanta Constitution had recently done a feature on Benji and reported his impending trip home, so people far and wide wanted to celebrate with the family.

"So much for a quiet visit home," Benji chuckled as he wiped tears, saluted to folks, and mouthed *thank you's*. He felt overwhelmed by the way people he didn't even know had turned out to honor him. All along the way, people would run alongside the car as far as they could keep up. Then fresh runners would take over. As they neared Smytheville city limits, the throngs had grown. Benji kept waving and saluting, but suddenly he started recognizing the runners. A group of his high school teammates were with him. The tears came on with force when he recognized his tightest buddies from high school. There were T-Winy, Dog Hair, PeeWee, and Tadpole.

"Mom, you told me PeeWee had gotten into drugs. He looks great now." All the while, Benji was waving to his buddies and giving thumbs-ups.

"That's a story for later. Too long to tell just now, but I'll just say your bravery played a big part in his getting clean. I'll catch you up on the others too."

People stood four and five deep, some on flatbed trucks. They were chanting, "Welcome home, Hero, welcome home." Benji began seeing people he knew – school buddies, church family, business men, close friends. Then he started seeing the red, white, and blue decorations on each light pole. Flags lined the median. Banners overhead read *Benji, our hero, home at last.*

There were no dry eyes in the car. Even though Molly, Thad, and Belinda were aware there would be a welcome home ceremony, a few days later, they had no idea people would respond like this.

"Could we stop and let me get out and thank everybody?"

Thad spoke up. "Benji, you've had about enough for your first sight of home today. Just roll your window down and yell your thanks; tell them you will see them Saturday. That will give you a couple of days to rest up before the big welcome home."

"You mean this isn't it?" Benji was totally overwhelmed. "This is a real hero's welcome, and I don't feel like I'm a hero."

Thad answered, "That's one of the reasons you are, Son."

Again, Benji got a lump in his throat at Thad's calling him *Son.*

Molly told him, "Well, apparently the town feels differently, Benji. They have planned a huge welcome home party set for you on Saturday. I suggest you just accept the accolades graciously. So many feel you have taken the injuries in their place because they couldn't go and fight. The whole town has prayed for you daily, and this is their chance to say thank you to you and to God. Let them celebrate."

Benji rolled his window down, pulled himself halfway out of the car and yelled, "Thank you, thank you, thank you. I'll see you Saturday."

Smytheville had never seen such fanfare as Saturday held – bands, mounted riders, horns blaring, street vendors, and hordes of people. It appeared all Smytheville had turned out as well as many from neighboring towns.

After the mayor quieted the five-minute ovation, Benji, in his dress uniform, slowly mounted the platform. Thad supported him on one side just to be certain he didn't fall, and then went to his seat with the family after Benji was safely on stage. The crowd exploded with cheers once again. They only quieted when Benji began to speak:

"Thank you, once again, for your prayers and support. I'm so humbled by the outpouring of love I have received from this community, but I don't deserve this. People call me hero, but I'm not the hero. My buddies who are still fighting every day, knowing their lives may be cut short any minute, those who risked their own lives giving me first aid and dragging me out of harm's way, those soldiers who gave the ultimate sacrifice – those are the heroes."

"Since I returned home, many have asked what my feelings are about what I've been through, did I regret having to go to Afghanistan, if I had any resentment against our government who got us into the battle, did I have bitterness about my injuries? My answer is sincere. The only regret I have is that I didn't get to finish the job, and that I can't go back and fight with my guys. I think of them every day. Most of you know I played high school and college basketball. I learned of teamwork there, but nothing compares to the camaraderie – the bond – that exists on the battlefield. You may not even like the guy next to you; he may get on your last nerve, but the worst man in the platoon – the one you may detest most – he's still your brother in the fight and you would die for him and he would for you."

"As far as my disabilities, I learned from a friend - a one-armed surgeon – that the only disability anyone faces is the one between the ears. He told me you can do the same things you did before; you just have to figure out new ways to do them. So to T-Winy, Dog Hair, PeeWee, Tadpole, you better get in shape because I can outrun you, even if it's in a wheelchair and I know I can out-shoot you still. I'll see you on the court."

After being presented with numerous awards, the crowd was invited to stay for the cookout. Benji had a seat of honor and talked at length with the many that came by. But Benji couldn't stay seated when a one-eyed, slumped-shouldered, ninety-year-old, decorated veteran, decked out in his baggy uniform, came up saluting him. Benji struggled to get up, saluted the soldier and thanked him for his service. Tears ran down both their faces with an unspoken understanding of what the other had been through.

A Shocking Visitor

After returning home and exhilarated by the day's events, Benji had used all his energy and felt wiped out. It didn't take a doctor nor a nurse to see he badly needed some rest; a mother could discern it quickly.

"Benji, why don't you lie down for a while? I will field all the congratulatory calls and thank them for you. I'll keep a list of names and phone numbers. If and when you choose, you can call them back. You may not be able to sleep; I know the adrenalin is flowing from this wonderful day of celebration, but just close your eyes and relax; it will help you. I know you still don't have all your strength back and if you overtire, it will make you more susceptible to infections. I'll get you up in time for supper."

When Benji stretched out, he patted the bed beside him. "Mom, come sit here a minute; I want to ask you something."

Molly did as he requested.

"Mom, you said you would tell me about PeeWee. I really want to know all that's transpired. I know PeeWee has always been troubled, but he has been such a faithful friend to me."

"Benji, this conversation will take more than a minute. Why don't you take your respite while I put on a one-pot dinner that can cook until we are ready to eat? After you have rested, we'll find a private place, and I will tell you the entire scenario."

"Okay. Will do. You've always told me, 'Mother knows best.'" He smiled that teasing endearing grin. With that, Benji closed his eyes and his exhaustion demanded sleep.

After two hours, Benji awakened and felt as though he was arousing from a coma. He had completely surrendered to the rest his body had commanded. He called out to Molly. Here in the bedroom, they could have their conversation about PeeWee undisturbed.

Molly pulled the bedroom chair near where Benji lay. "Benji, after you left for the army, your old group, more or less, dissolved. All of them, except PeeWee found their niche in life. Surprising enough, Tadpole hit it better than any of them. He landed a job with the post office, making more money than he could ever have imagined. God smiled on him by giving him a girl who not only loved him, but looked up to him as her prince. They married and have made a great home. They are faithful in their church.

T-Winey always enjoyed tinkering with cars and making them go as fast as streaks of lightening. That got him into a little trouble along the way – many citations and one so steep he had to do a little jail time. He was going 95 in a school zone. Nonetheless, he is now doing what he loves. He is a mechanic down at the Toyota dealership. He keeps up on all the new car developments and is so good at what he does, other dealerships are trying to lure him away, but Toyota is paying him so well in salary and unbelievable benefits, he'll never go anywhere else.

Dog Hair worked at several minimum-waged jobs, and finally saw he needed some education. He enrolled in our local junior college. He struggled there but made it through. He now manages McDonald's. He was married to Fran Sessions for a couple of years, but she divorced him, looking for greener pastures.

Benji didn't interrupt her, but had gotten a few letters from some of his pals and others at home that gave him some of this info. Strangely enough, not a word about PeeWee had ever been mentioned. "Mom, what about PeeWee?"

"If you remember, PeeWee never talked much about his family. There was a reason. His dad Buster abused him, his little sister, and his mom. They lived on a small renter farm just a couple of miles out of town. PeeWee floundered for a while, going from one construction job to the next. He was always just a grunt, taking materials to the carpenters. He would mix mortar for the brick layers and do any other menial task he was asked to do. He never made enough to move out on his own and was always afraid to because he had come between his dad's fist and his mother's cheek many times. He feared what might happen to her if he left. He did most of the outside chores on the farm and gave his dad a generous portion of his meager pay check to shut him up about him being a free-loader.

He came home from work one day to find his dad dragging his little sister into one of the outside sheds. He knew his large, muscular dad was up to no good and could tell by his stagger that he had drunk more than a couple of beers. His daddy was mean but became nothing short of a villain when he drank too much.

PeeWee had taken all kinds of abuse from his dad as he was growing up, including verbal humiliation because he wasn't muscular like him. Knowing he would be no match for his physical strength, but realizing he had to stop whatever cruelty Buster was about to inflict on Missy, PeeWee went in the house and pulled the rifle off the gun rack above the mantle.

When he neared the shed, he could hear Missy's screams and pleadings. He also heard the disgusting, vulgar slurred replies from his dad. He ran then to help Missy. When he opened the door, he saw them both naked from the waist down and his sorry excuse of a father on top of her having his way. With no hesitation, PeeWee shot his dad in the back from fairly close range. The shot hit its mark through the heart.

After wrapping Missy in a nearby feed sack to cover his little sister's nakedness so as to avoid her further humiliation, he took her in his arms to offer what comfort he could.

When the sheriff arrived, before he bothered to get the full details, he asked PeeWee if he had shot his dad. PeeWee proudly answered, 'I did. I gave the bastard what he deserved.' His mother had come and taken Missy in the house before the sheriff had arrived.

'Boy, that's murder,' the sheriff declared. 'We're taking you in.'

The hotheaded sheriff didn't want to hear anything PeeWee had to say and was infuriated because he had shot his poker pal, one who still owed him $500.

After a hearing, the facts surfaced and PeeWee was exonerated. But the damage was done. PeeWee struggled with the injustice he had experienced, the anger he had about his little sister being violated, and with his unjustified guilt from killing his dad.

Knowing his mom and Missy wouldn't be harmed anymore, PeeWee disappeared for a couple of months. Some said he was over in Atlanta. There he experienced some drugs. He liked the numbness they gave him. So as drug use often does, one led to another, one just a little more powerful than the previous one. He ended up jobless because he stayed in a drugged stupor. I heard he was homeless, sleeping on the streets, and stealing to pay for his drug habit. All of that was so hard to believe until one day shortly after Christmas.

Everyone had gone home and Thad was away on a medical mission trip up the Amazon. I wanted to go too, but he said the accommodations were too rugged for women. So I stayed at home and took down Christmas decorations. I had been in and out of the house that day, so I hadn't bothered setting the alarm; I hadn't even locked the doors. It was a Wednesday, so I had put a halt to my day's work to get ready for midweek bible study and weekly prayer meeting. I had just gotten out of the shower and had gotten into my underwear when I was surprised by a cold knife blade at my throat.
You can imagine what situations entered my mind – rape, robbery, murder – you name it.

The man said, 'Ma'am, you do just what I say and you won't get hurt.' The masked intruder threw me on the bed and tied up my hands and feet. All the while, I was praying. Then my mind fixated on what he had said – 'Ma'am.' So polite in tone and that voice – it was too familiar.

I began to pray aloud. 'Father, please help me, please help this man who seems intent on doing harm. Please make him see the error of his ways and seek your face. Father I forgive him even before he harms me because that's what you have told us to do – that's what you did when men beat you, spit on you, and nailed you to a cross. How can I do any less? Make my heart pliable so I will be more concerned about him than about my own well-being.'

Silence filled the room, except for audible crying, not from me, but from the intruder. I was more than shocked when the man sat down by me on the bed. When he threw off his mask, I could barely recognize PeeWee. Drugs had so changed his appearance and personality, it was unbelievable.

'Oh, Ms. Molly, I'm so very sorry. I thought I could do this. I knew you would have money here and this was the best place I could think of to get my next fix.' Tears streamed down his dirty, scarred face. 'I should have known this is what you would do. I could take it if you had lashed out at me, but no, you had to pray, not just for yourself, but for me. Ms. Molly, I've made so many mistakes. God could never forgive me for all I've done. My life is neither worth saving nor worth yours or God's forgiveness.'

Please untie me and let's discuss this, PeeWee, and hand me a robe from the dresser over there.

Peewee even shielded his eyes as though he wanted now to let me have some modesty and said, 'Oh, I'm sorry. I would never have hurt you. You are the best, kindest woman I've ever known.'

Benji, we sat and talked for three hours. We had our own private prayer meeting. PeeWee poured out confession upon confession of his evil deeds, not the least was that of shooting his own dad. I explained that God didn't hold him accountable for defending Missy and He could and would forgive him of any and all of his sins, but that sin exacted a price and he would have to pay it.

'Go ahead and call the police. I know this can't go unpunished.'

'PeeWee,' I said to him, 'we all deserve a second chance. I'll make a deal with you. If you will go to rehab, one that Thad and I will arrange and pay for, and get clean, we will keep the law out of this. You can't do this by yourself, but God will help you. In addition, Thad and I will support you. You know if Benji can handle his physical rehab, you can endure whatever drug rehab requires.'

'You do know Benji is my hero and has always been. Every time I think of quitting this miserable life and shooting myself, I will remember what he has gone through and is going through.' He then reached over with a sincere embrace. Molly could feel his body trembling. She knew he was badly needing a fix. 'I'll do whatever you say. I really want to change, if you think there's a chance for me.'

This is a life's do-over, PeeWee; it's a new beginning.

'Ms. Molly, please get me in some place safe before I even leave your house. I'm already in such need of a fix, I'm afraid what I would do to someone else to get it.'

PeeWee, I'll have to call in some favors to get you situated, but I think I can get you in the hospital psych ward until we find the right facility. Right now, you go to the kitchen and cut yourself a piece of the chocolate cake that's on the counter. Milk is in the fridge. You're at home in my kitchen. Let me get dressed and I will be there shortly.

Benji, by that time he was shaking so badly I knew he had to have help fast.

'One other thing, PeeWee,' I told him in a sterner voice, 'if you leave, I WILL call the law and all bets will be off.'

PeeWee then endured and completed rigorous rehab. His road to sobriety was not an easy one because he had been so deeply addicted. He even refused to leave the first time they declared him clean. He said he knew he would just go out and jump into the same pigpen. He knew he was still too weak to stay clean. After months of rehab and counseling, the rehab officials told him he HAD to get out in the real world to see how strong he was. Our pastor had counseled him each week and encouraged him to pray every day for his supernatural strength.

Thad and I talked with a friend in construction and asked him to give PeeWee a chance. He did. He told me that he had never had a better, more dependable worker and that he was making him an apprentice to his bricklayers. 'This will give him a well-paying skill that will take him through life,' reported Joe, the construction friend.

The end of the story is that we have a weekly accountability meeting with PeeWee every week. This is part of his self-imposed rehab.

Family Time

Respecting the fact Benji still needed much rest, Molly decided to wait a couple of days before having the big family dinner. The whole gang was there – Molly, Thad, Caitlin, Bob, Emily, Celeste, Belinda, Benji and the adopted family members - Sawyer and Gloria.

As usual, Molly had the table so heavily laden with good eats, it was in danger of collapsing. "Mom, I wish you had cooked something I could eat," Benji teased. She had made a point of having all his favorites. The chatter was so continual, it was difficult to center on any one of the many conversations taking place at one time. Everybody was trying to ask Benji questions – "What happened the day you were shot?" "What has been the most difficult thing you've had to deal with?" "Are you still in pain?" "When will you be released from the hospital permanently?" "How does your prosthesis work?"

Benji finally called a time-out. "Although it may have been indirectly, you have heard the answers to these questions many times over. I'd like to catch up on what's going on with everyone else, but could we do it one at a time, PLEASE? I'm

171

ready for my identity to be more than my injuries."

Caitlin waved her raised arm in school girl fashion. "I want to go first. I've waited to tell you until you got home, but Beau will have a new cousin in about seven months. I know he will enjoy having a playmate at family gatherings." Ever since the day of the church invader and Bob's acknowledging to Caitlin that he knew and had forgiven her of any indiscretions, their marriage had taken on a more genuine love than ever before. When the two looked at each other, nothing but adoration was visible.

"And I hadn't said anything, but I was just thinking you had been eating too much of Mom's cooking. Really, I think this is great. Miss Emily, what do you think about getting a little brother?"

"It will be a l-o-n-g time though, Uncle Benji. That's what my mommy tells me every time I ask."

"And she asks no less than fifty times a day," Caitlin said.

Benji loved teasing his niece and picking at his sister. "Emily, I'll bet if you will ask more often, Mommy will get it here sooner."

"Benji Pate, you are as mean as ever," said Caitlin. Then, with great warmth said, "But you don't know how much I've missed our banter while you've been away." She took her napkin and wiped her tears away.

Celeste chimed in with the same jovial spirit, "What I've really missed, Benji, has been your contribution to our regular covered-dish family meals – your generous and time-consuming offering of Milo's sweet tea." That brought laughter from the entire group.

Sawyer and Gloria told him about their recent nuptials. "Gloria now is officially Mrs. Thomas. Since she is Celeste's mom, and Celeste is your half-sister, I guess that makes us officially part of the family."

Celeste spoke up. "I guess this is the time I should announce I have found my life's love."

"Who is he, what does he do, when can I meet him?" Benji had a list of questions.

"His name is Dr. Ferrell Patton. He recently completed his residency in general surgery and is on staff at Georgia Baptist. As to when you can meet him, I don't know. I didn't want to bring him this weekend because we had so much going on, and I wanted nothing to take the spotlight off Benji." With an exaggerated shiver, she said, "Ferrell is so handsome no one would be able to look at anyone or anything other than him."

"Well, Miss Priss," Benji said addressing his half-sister, "I'll bet Belinda and I will beat you down the aisle. They tell me my rehab may take six months to a year. We have discussed it and want to tie the knot as soon as I get back home. We have opted for a simple family wedding here in the back yard. All of you are invited." No clarification was needed about Beau and Belinda's situation. Molly had explained it to the family when they had taken Belinda into their home.

Cheers broke out from around the table. With that, Beau was awakened. Belinda got him out of his crib and brought him in so he could see the source of the hullabaloo.

Lastly, Thad spoke up and said with trembling, tearful voice. "I just want to tell you one more time how thankful I am to be a part of this family, and, Benji, I don't think I've ever prayed for anyone as much as I have for your healing. I can't quit thanking God for sparing your life and bringing you back to us. Thank you, once again, for your service and sacrifice. I know that your suffering will not be in vain. God can, will, and already has used it for good."

"Thanks, Thad. Tell me about your recent mission trip down the Amazon." Benji inserted, trying to draw the emotional attention away from him.

Again, Thad's emotions got the best of him. Tears trickled down his cheeks as he tried to give Benji the good news. "Benji, I've never seen people so eager to hear about Jesus. We would get off the boat and go back through the brush to remote villages. We would show the Jesus movie and our pastor preached through a translator. When the plan of salvation was given, people flocked to the temporary altar we erected to pray to accept Christ. I got to personally present the plan of salvation and pray for more people than I could ever have imagined. At the end of our ten-day trip, over 3,000 souls were saved. This trip with Amazon Hope* has changed me forever. I can't wait to go back."

"Let me tell you a testimony of our leader, Ty Harris. This newly formed team went down the first street of the village of Ashini and came to a home where a boy with cerebral palsy lived. Ty was the only one in the group with training and experience with children with disabilities, and he was able to teach this family how to better care for the little boy. Ty said, 'The time and place were designed by God because it was through our luggage being left behind that we even went to that village. That wasn't on our original itinerary. Through this, family members gave their hearts to Christ.'"

"Maybe I can go with you some day," said Benji.

The serious moment was interrupted by the ringing of the house phone. "I'll get it," said Molly. "Belinda, it's for you."

"Who in the world would be calling me here tonight?" Belinda arose from her chair with a puzzled look. Although she answered the phone in the other room, Benji could see Belinda from where he was sitting and noticed her countenance change from joy to fear.

"Who was that?" he asked when she returned to the table.

"Ah, it was just some prankster trying to scare me." She waved her hand dismissing his concern. "It was nothing. Let's not let some idiot destroy our evening." Although Benji discerned her nonchalance was artificial, she tried to continue pleasant conversation.

After dinner, the crowd dispersed. "Let's walk out back and see just where our wedding ceremony will be – you know, like where we'll set up chairs, where the altar will be and stuff like that," Benji suggested to Belinda. They walked around, arm in arm, enjoying the cool of the evening. "Belinda, there's one thing we need to clear up. If we are going to join our lives forever, let's make one mutual promise – no more secrets between us – ever. Now tell me about the earlier call."

"Benji, I didn't want to put a damper on things, and it probably was just hot air."

"Who was it?"

"Dirk, the double jerk."

"What did he say? I want to know right now." Benji's agitation showed not only in words, but also how he grabbed Belinda and glared into her eyes.

"I don't want you to worry about anything while your home. Let's just forget it and pass it off as his blowing off."

"That's not going to happen, Belinda. Tell me every word and tell me now."

"He's making some threats," she stammered with tears in her eyes. "I want to believe he is just drunk and blowing smoke, but he said there was no way he would allow ---. I don't want to say it." Belinda buried her face in her hands and started sobbing.

"What? What did he say?"

"He said there was no way a Crip was going to be a father to his son. That he was going to take me to court for parental rights."

Anger boiled in Benji's eyes. "That sorry... No curse words are expressive enough to describe him. He didn't want to admit to paternity when he raped you and impregnated you. He let you go through all this alone, and now he wants to step in. I'll tell you one thing for certain — that's not about to happen. Where was he?"

"I don't know, Benji. It was loud. Probably some bar. Let's let it go. It probably meant nothing," she cried.

"I'm not letting it go. I'll take care of it right now. "

Major Confrontation

Benji started back into the house to get his mom's car keys, only to realize he had not advanced to driving with his prosthesis. He reached into his pocket for his cell phone and dialed the numbered Tadpole had left on his phone earlier. "Tad, I need some help. Come and get me."

"I'll be there in five." Tad didn't even ask what it was about. If Benji needed anything, he always had his back.

"Belinda," Benji said as he held her tightly. "I want you to go back in, make excuses for me – maybe say that Tadpole came by and wanted me to go riding with him for a while – anything, but don't say anything to the others about what's going on."

"Benji, I really don't want you doing this. P-l-e-a-s-e just let it pass. I believe it was just drunk talk. I don't want you to get hurt. Dirk is not worth it."

"Me, get hurt?' he huffed. "You had better be saying your prayers for the jerk. I know he's not worth it, but you are. I'm not having him messing with you in any way anymore."

Belinda was still pleading for him not to go as he rode off with Tad. "Take me to the

Fuzzy Duck first, Tad. That's probably the jerks hang out."

"What is going on? I know you don't drink. Who's the jerk? Tell me what we're doing, friend."

Benji gave Tad an abbreviated version and told him he didn't want him involved. "Just drive me and stay in the car."

"You know that's not happening. I've always enjoyed participating in a good fight. You ain't going in there alone."

"I'm not going in to fight, just to talk."

"Well, I'm going in to talk, too, then."

As soon as they entered, from the bar came a raucous laugh. "Well if it isn't our hero," slurred Dirk. "I called your girl, and I knew you'd come a-running, Crip." he smirked and patted the guy next to him on the back.

Before Tadpole's strides reached him, about two or three guys had already swung. The guy who had been next to him had socked Dirk right in the nose. He picked him up off the floor, held him by the collar and shouted into his face, "Drunk or not, you aren't disrespecting one who has risked his life and lost his leg for your freedom."

By then Benji got into the middle of the fray and said, "Guys, thanks for your support, but I just want to talk to Dirk. Why don't you come outside with me and let me explain a few things," directing his comments to Dirk.

With blood still running down the front of his shirt, Dirk's bravado was worse than ever. "Just say whatever you've got to say right here. You want to tell these guys how you've hooked up with Belinda, the whore? She is as easy as melted butter. I had my way with her, but so did half the town."

Benji drew back to waylay him, but before he could balance enough to do it, Tadpole walloped him. "Let's go, Benji, before the cops come and haul this piece of --- off."

"I'm not through, Dirk. I want to have my say when you are sober."

Tad pulled Benji out the door. He had been there before and knew those other guys weren't through with Dirk yet.

By the time they returned, the house was quiet. The only light was outside where Belinda sat wringing her hands. Tad let Benji out and told him to call again if he needed him. Benji told Belinda only part of the scenario. "I'm not finished with him, but I can promise you one thing. He will never bother you again."

Dirk No Longer A Problem

Benji's cell phone rang early the next morning. He grabbed it from his nightstand and answered it, hoping it wouldn't wake anyone else.

"Problem solved," announced Tad. "Go get the paper."

"Tad, it takes me a while to get my legs on and get my day started. Why don't you just tell me what you're talking about?"

"You'll see soon enough. Benji, just ask no questions."

Benji couldn't wait to start the morning process of getting up and geared up with his prosthesis. When he did, he started out the front door to pick up the paper, only to hear Thad say, "Good Morning, Benji. For staying out late, you are up early."

Benji saw that Thad had already retrieved the paper and was past the A section and to the sports section. "I just awoke early. Old habits are hard to break. Nurses usually wake me earlier than this with morning meds and vitals checks. I just thought I would go out to get the paper, but I see you beat me to it."

"Come in and have a seat. I'll share it with you."

Benji found a comfortable chair and delved into the front page. Front and center was a picture of a wrecker which had a twisted chunk of metal still half way off a cliff. The headline jumped out at him – 'Drunk driver missed curve, one dead.' He knew without reading further who that was. Sure enough, Dirk would never bother them again.

Problem Solved

Now that danger of further harassment was over, Benji and Belinda discussed the situation and felt it only fair to share with Molly and Thad, at breakfast, the situation that had shaken them to the core.

"Was that why you left with Tadpole last night? To see what you could do?" Thad asked.

"It was and it was something I shouldn't have done. Tad and I went to the bar for me to confront Dirk and let him know he needed to back off and leave us alone. Dirk was drunk, and I learned in the army how useless it is to try to reason with one. Tad was trying to take up for me and keep me out of a fray, so he and Dirk had a scuffle."

"Oh, no," interjected Molly. "How badly did that turn out?"

"There wasn't much to it. Even the guys who were with Dirk let him know he was way out of line. But that is all water under the bridge. I guess Dirk did himself in, so we won't have to deal with him anymore. It will suit me just fine if Beau only knows me as his father. I would hate for him to ever think he had Dirk's evil blood in him."

Time was zooming by and there were wedding details Benji and Belinda needed to see to before he had to return to the hospital. Belinda drove him to see a caterer, to arrange for the outdoor altar arch, and a few other unexciting chores. "You're being unusually quiet today, Benji," Belinda said as she glanced his way. "Are you feeling okay, or is all this too much for you?"

"No, no. It's nothing like that. In fact all this running around helps get my mind off other things, and with the wedding less than two months away, I want to help what I can to get things ready."

Belinda looked his way and raised her eyebrows to question.

"It's nothing to worry about. I just have a niggling of uneasiness. I'm not sure why. Let's forget it and let nothing mar this happy time."

Belinda really wanted to query him more but somehow agreed to let it rest and just be happy.

"You only have two more days before you go back. Do you want to get with some of your friends for a night out, or is there anything else you would like to do?"

"Not unless they call. I really had rather spend this time with you and Beau. Could I have a date to take the two of you out tonight? I know mom will want to have a family meal the last night to send me off full and fat."

"Oh, that would be great. As much as I love your family and friends, we haven't had much "us" time. I look forward to it."

For the remainder of the day, Benji put on a happy face, but there were times Belinda caught a glimpse of him staring off in deep thought. Once a police car slowed down as it passed the house. Belinda noticed Benji tensing up, but she knew him well enough to leave it alone until he was ready to talk about it.

"Belinda, I've made reservations for us for 6:30 at Down Under, that new steakhouse. Does that suit you?"

"That's great. I've wanted to try it out. I guess I need to put Beau down for a nap so he will be in good shape for our date."

"I think I'll go over to Tadpole's for a bit while you and Beau nap. I want him to be my best man at the wedding."

"Who will drive you?"

"I keep forgetting I can't drive yet. I'll call PeeWee; he's told me a blue jillion times since I've been home to call him if I needed to go someplace."

Belinda didn't comment more, even though Benji's downcast eyes made questionable his excuse for going there.

There was more than he was saying about last night's incident.

When PeeWee picked Benji up, Benji told him, "PeeWee, I want to ask a big favor. Will you just drop me off at Tadpole's place and let me call you when I get ready to go home? I have a private matter to discuss with him."

"Sure, but what's with all the mystery. I saw Tad last night and he was acting all weird. He was jumpy every time a car slowed down. It was like he was expecting somebody."

Benji altered the truth a bit to shake off any doubt. "I just have some wedding stuff to discuss with him, and you know Tadpole. He can get all antsy about nothing."

Tadpole met Benji at the door as though he was expecting him. "Hi, Benji. What brings you out slumming?"

"I just needed to talk with you."

"What was the last thing I said to you this morning?" answering his own question, Tadpole sternly repeated, "Ask no questions."

"Okay, but you just tell me then. Patrol cars are slowing down at my place. You are antsy about something. Just tell me."

"I'll tell you all you need to know. Dirk's family heard about the fracas at the bar and asked that his accident be investigated.

The police have questioned his buddies and me. We all told them the same thing. Dirk was crazy drunk that night and there was no talking him out of doing what he wanted to do. His companions even told the police they had tried to take his keys away from him. We told them about the disrespect he showed you. The officers were in total agreement with our defense of you. They started to come question you, but we told them you had been through enough. They accepted our statements and said that would be the end of the investigation. So there you have it. Nothing for you to worry about so let it go."

"Pal, I thank you for everything. I just didn't want you to be in any trouble. I guess I need to call PeeWee to pick me up now, but one more thing. Would you stand up for me one more time – that is at the wedding? I want you to be my best man."

Tadpole was shocked and overcome with humility. "I don't feel worthy to stand up for you, to stand by you, or anything else, but it would truly be my honor."

Benji returned to Belinda with a fresh sparkle in his eyes. He was finally at ease. Their evening out was just what they needed. A good meal, followed by intimate conversation, which they had had little time for since he had been home. "Belinda, I just want you to know I love you more today than

I did yesterday, and it's my prayer that I will renew that statement every day of our lives together."

"Benji Pate, you are the best thing that has ever happened to me. You are noble, true, faithful, and caring, but best of all, you are mine." Then she used lyrics from an old Johnny Mathis song, "I will love you 'til the twelfth of never"

Benji responded in kind, "And that's a long, long time." After staring at each other with love beaming from their eyes for long minutes, they heard a slight snore. They looked over to see Beau's sleepy head down in his plate.

"I think that is our cue to call it a night and get this young man to bed," said Benji.

Another Kind of Uneasiness

After the family had enjoyed their big celebratory dinner, Caitlin had helped Molly clear the table and clean the kitchen. She took this opportunity to bend her mother's ear about her own concerns. "Mom, I've wanted to talk with you for a while now, but so much has been going on with Benji, I haven't wanted to bother you."

"What's going on? Even though you have taken part in all the festivities and acted as though you were as overjoyed as everyone else, I've sensed part of it has been a cover for something troubling you. You know, you can't hide everything from your mom. You and Bob are okay, aren't you?"

"I guess things are better with Bob and me than they have ever been. That's not it. It's the baby. The doctor spotted something unusual on his kidney on the sonogram. He keeps telling me he thinks it's nothing to worry about, but you must know how hard it is to put it out of my mind. Something keeps nagging me. I'm so afraid God is going to punish me for my sin by giving this baby some deformity." Tears filled Caitlin's eyes.

"Remind me, sweetie. Didn't you ask God to forgive you?"

"Well, yes," Caitlin said with some hesitation.

"Do you believe He can?"

"Certainly."

"But do you believe He did?"

"I know He did."

"Then, why don't you put that thought about God punishing you as far away as God did your iniquity?"

"You always make me see things clearer, Mom. Maybe that's just another reason why I love you so."

"Caitlin, I do think it would be a good idea if you tell this to Thad – about the sonogram, not the other – and ask him to take a look at the pictures. He will either dismiss it as a fluke as your obstetrician did, or he will put you with the right person for another opinion. You know Thad will be taking a long, hard look at it because he is almost as excited about this grandchild as I am. Peace of mind is worth a great deal. In the meantime, let's make this a matter of prayer. If God can make Alzheimer's disappear, he can make a little spot on a picture disappear." They both nodded in agreement.

"Let's pray now, Mom."

Later, Caitlin found Thad in his study alone. She did as Molly suggested and showed him the sonogram pictures her doctor had allowed her to bring. Thad studied them

191

with a furrowed brow. Caitlin's hands were sweaty as she waited for his pronouncement that something was bad wrong with her baby boy. Finally, he raised his head up and gave her a comforting smile. "Young lady, I really think you need to put every worry out of your mind. I believe you have a healthy baby. My best bet is there was a speck on the camera. This doesn't look like any abnormal growth I've ever seen."

Caitlin couldn't contain her joy. This time her tears were drops of joy. She went behind Thad's desk and gave him the biggest bear hug her growing belly would allow. "You don't know how reassuring your assessment is, Thad. My doctor said it was nothing to worry about, but when someone who has a family connection says the same thing, it just means more. I love you."

A New Beginning

The weeks of rehab flew by like a breeze, but not without a few glitches. Benji had started getting a pressure sore at one point, but according to Joyce's instructions, he reported it quickly. A few days with the prosthesis off and aggressive treatment, all was well. Joyce made the slight adjustments needed to prevent it from happening again, he hoped. Again he warned Benji to be diligent in reporting any problem. "That's the only way we can fix it; otherwise, you can get a severe infection that will set you back a lot longer."

Benji put every ounce of energy into his tasks. With great determination, he learned to walk on his prosthesis. He accomplished navigating stairs, but best of all, he passed the driving test.

"By the way, Joyce – you did say to call you by your first name – you once told me you would tell me the rest of your story."

"It's certainly not a pretty tale, but I guess you might be interested in hearing it. After I lost my leg to a motorcycle accident – not exactly the heroic way you lost yours – I became bitter. I was angry with God. Today I know God didn't put me on that dangerous machine. Nor did he tell me to drive recklessly, but then I needed to blame someone besides myself. I know I don't hold single rights to that reaction, but that was just the way it was. I started drinking heavily and staying out late. My wife was left with the main responsibility of raising our only son. He was a teenager and needed the stern hand of his dad, but I just wasn't there emotionally for him. Physically, it wasn't much more of my time he got. I was too caught up in my own anger and self-pity. I loved him, but I'm not sure he knew it. It was neither my nature to vocalize love to him nor to my wife. I've learned how important it is to say it and to hear it since then."

"All this sounds like past tense. What happened with him, Joyce?"

"He took a page from my book. If it was okay for his old man to get soused every night, what was wrong with his drinking, he reasoned. One night he was out with some of his pals, and I assume they all had had too much to drink. They ran off an embankment and all were killed except my son Joel, and Joel's injuries were life-threatening. He was airlifted to UAB Hospital. On our sixty-five mile drive there, I could see such hurt in my wife's eyes, I knew she blamed me. I prayed all the way, sometimes silently and sometimes crying out to God audibly. Why would a God on whom I had turned my back ever listen to me? But I begged him anyway to spare our son. I bargained with him. 'Lord, if you will just let Joel live, I'll never drink again. I'll be the father to him I should have been for the past years.'"

"Apparently that wasn't good enough for God. Now I know He wanted me to turn back to him unconditionally. But that knowledge came to me several years later. When we arrived at the ER, the doctor came out with that look that told all. They couldn't save our son. The injuries were just too massive."

"That only made me angrier at God, and his death and my continued drinking finished off our marriage. Sue had put up with all she intended to and held me responsible for our son's deadly end. To be truthful, I secretly blamed myself too."

"But, Joyce, that doesn't seem to be who you are today. What changed you?"

"That's another long story, but let's just says God has infinite patience and mercy. After about five more years of self-destructive lifestyle, he put Rachael, a prosthetist, in my path. She worked with me to get a prosthesis that fit properly and with my reporting discomfort early enough to avoid many infections. She cut me no slack and didn't tolerate my occasional rants against God. She was a strong Christian and

195

would tell me in no uncertain terms that she wouldn't listen to my blaming Him for my problems. 'You have to own up to your own contributions to your situation,' she would say. 'You do know God lost a son too, for your sins and mine.' Long story short, she convinced me to go to church with her a few times. I couldn't sit under the sound of the gospel and keep telling myself that God was to blame for everything. We've been married now for three years, and God and Rachael have given me a new beginning."

"Wow!" said Benji, "I guess God just wasn't ready to turn you loose. I'll have to remember your story when I want to blame God."

"That is the only reason I share it. I believe I owe it to God to tell about His grace."

Benji's only disappointment during these days back at Walter Reed was the absence of his old friend Dr. Newell. He resigned himself to the fact that he had forever burned the bridge in their relationship.

During his days away, Belinda put the final touches on the wedding particulars, with Molly's help. Decisions had been endless, but the results of their efforts prepared for a flawless wedding.

Late October gave Benji and Belinda a weather-perfect day for their wedding. The temperature had cooled after an unbearably hot summer. The red, yellow, and golden leaves provided a dazzling background for an outdoor wedding.

It was always a celebration when the family congregated, but this day was super-energized with love. The backyard overflowed with many friends, as well as family. Breaking with all tradition of staying out of sight until the march down the aisle, Benji and Belinda, instead, circulated among the many attendees and gloried in every minute of the day. Shortly before time for them to get in position for the wedding, Benji spotted two surprise visitors walking across the yard, Dr. Jeff and Susan Newell. Benji froze in surprise for a minute and then wanted to run, but knew he was not that proficient yet. Instead, both he and Dr. Newell walked at a rapid pace toward each other and embraced.

Jeff Newell whispered in Benji's ear, "Thanks buddy, for giving me the reality slap in the face no one had ever dared do before. When you painted such a clear picture of mine and Susan's true relationship – my adultery with my profession being my mistress, I thought I never wanted to see you again. You know, truth is the hardest thing to

197

hear and accept. But, it was the best thing that could have ever happened to me. I realized Susan wasn't the only one at fault. I want to tell you more after the ceremony. Go, now, and marry your bride."

Other surprise visitors showed up – Flo, Joyce and Rachael, Dr. and Mrs. Skelton. Benji had posted a blanket invitation for the staff, not really thinking any of them would show up. "I hope no one needs help at Walter Reed today. I think most of the staff is here."

"Well, the best part of the staff is here anyway," teased Dr. Skelton. You had better be glad some had to stay back and work, or you wouldn't have had enough food. None of the ones who worked with you, Benji, wanted to miss this day. You became one of our star patients. At least those left behind sent gifts."

"I even loved you on your grouchy days," added Flo.

Benji thought his heart might burst with joy. What a great way to begin a new life with the woman he loved and also to have so many wonderful people in his life there to help celebrate!

When he saw Belinda coming down the aisle on Thad's arm and Beau holding Thad's other hand, he recognized a beauty in Belinda beyond what he had ever seen before.

He knew God had to have designed this day and this union. This truly was a high and holy moment.

When the minister asked, "Who gives this women to be wed?" as only a toddler could, Beau stole the show when he said, "Papa Thad and I do."

Just before the couple began saying their vows, Emily broke the silence with her exclamation. "Mom, you are peeing your pants. It's running down your legs and all over the grass!"

The photographer had to snap a picture to record the open-mouthed shock on Caitlin's face. There she stood by the bride in her matron of honor frilly, peach-colored dress realizing her water had just broken.

"You did it again, Sis," Benji joked. "You just had to steal the show." Laughter filled the yard, an appropriate response for comedian Benji.

Flo, who had just met Emily, spoke up and said, "Let the show go on. Emily and I have this." In her sweet way of handling situations, she led Emily into the house, with an overwhelmed Bob following behind. "Emily, have your contractions started?"

"No, nothing but just this embarrassing wetness."

"We'll find you something dry in a minute, but I feel sure we have ample time to watch them say their vows." The two watched the wedding out the window before taking care of other pressing needs.

As Benji and Belinda recited the vows each had so movingly written, Belinda added at the close, "Thank you, my love, for loving and accepting me, warts and all, just as my Heavenly Father already has. Benji Pate, I'll love you 'til the twelfth of never.'"

With happy tears streaming down his face, Benji replied, "And that's a long, long time."

After the ceremony, friends and family greeted the bride and groom. Finally Dr. Newell had his chance to talk at length to Benji about how his remarks had made him see the error of his ways, and how he and Susan had spent many hours with a Christian counselor. They had confessed to each other and to God their sins. "We prayed together; first, asking for God to forgive us and then praying we could forgive each other. We have a new beginning, just as you and Belinda now have."

"Isn't it fitting a new family member will begin his life just as you and Belinda begin yours as husband and wife." Molly said and assured Benji and Belinda she would call and tell them when their nephew arrived.

"Tell her we will be praying for her and the baby," said Belinda.

As they drove away with everyone shouting well wishes, the couple turned and saw the words written on the back windshield, "God bless this new beginning."

Author's Note

Perhaps you have never experienced God's forgiveness; perhaps you've never experienced the perfect peace that can only come from having a personal relationship with our Lord and Savior, Jesus Christ, but that can be remedied today. I won't lie and say with Jesus as your Lord, all your problems will go away, but just as it was with the characters you've met in this book, you will have an advocate to see you through whatever may come your way. Let me encourage you to walk down the following road-The Roman Road - for a new beginning for your life:

Roman Road to Salvation

By Kevin Haag

The Roman Road to salvation is a collection of verses from the book of Romans explaining God's free gift of eternal life. Follow these verses to learn why we need salvation, God's plan of salvation, how to receive salvation, God's promise of eternal life, and the results of salvation.

1st stop on the Roman Road to Salvation...

God Is The Creator Of Life

Romans 1:20-21: *"For since the creation of the world God's invisible qualities – his eternal power and divine nature – have been clearly seen, being understood from what has been made, so that men are without excuse. For although they knew God, they neither glorified him as God nor gave thanks to him, but their thinking became futile and their foolish hearts were darkened."* God reveals himself to us - His divine nature and personal qualities - through creation. We must acknowledge God as the Creator and sustainer of life.

2nd stop on the Roman Road to Salvation...

Why We Need Salvation – The Fact of Our Sin

Romans 3:23: *"For all have sinned and fall short of the glory of God."* We must recognize that we are sinners and that we do not meet God's perfect standards. Sin is serious in God's sight and includes thoughts, words and actions. All sin (i.e. hatred and lust) makes us sinners, not just the big, obvious sins like murder and adultery (Romans 5:12).

3rd stop on the Roman Road to Salvation...

Man's Inability

Romans 3:10: *"As it is written: There is no one righteous, not even one."* No one can earn right standing with God. We must understand that our good deeds or religion are unacceptable to God because our good works cannot cancel out our sin. For a view of man's sinful condition, read Romans 3:10-18.

4th stop on the Roman Road to Salvation...

The Penalty of Sin

Romans 6:23a: *"For the wages of sin is death."* God's holiness demands a penalty (consequence) for our sin, which is death. Eternal death is separation from God forever in Hell. God is a just God, and He demands punishment for every sin. Justice is getting what we deserve, because of our sin, we deserve death.

5th stop on the Roman Road to Salvation...

God's Plan of Salvation

Romans 5:8: *"But God demonstrates his own love for us in this: While we were still sinners, Christ died for us."* God sent His Son Jesus Christ to pay the penalty for our sin by dying on the cross. God is a God of mercy and He sent Jesus to take our sin upon Himself and the punishment we deserve. Mercy is not getting what we deserve, we deserve death, and Jesus took our place.

6th stop on the Roman Road to Salvation...

God's Promise of Eternal Life

Romans 6:23: *"For the wages of sin is death, but the gift of God is eternal life in Christ Jesus our Lord."* Eternal life is a free gift from God, there is nothing we can do to earn eternal life. Grace is getting what we don't deserve. Because of God's amazing grace, He has given us eternal life through Jesus Christ!

7th stop on the Roman Road to Salvation...

Man's Responsibility

Romans 10:9-10: *"That if you confess with your mouth, 'Jesus is Lord,' and believe in your heart that God raised him from the dead, you will be saved. For it is with your heart that you believe and are justified, and it is with your mouth that you confess and are saved."* We must believe that the Lord Jesus Christ is the Son of God who died for us on the cross, rose from the dead, and is Lord. We must put our trust in Jesus alone to make us right with God. Salvation involves believing in our hearts (inward belief) and an outward confession that Jesus is Lord.

Romans 10:13: *"For everyone who calls on the name of the Lord will be saved."* There is no complicated formula to salvation; Jesus paid the price of our sin for us. Our response is to accept Jesus as our Lord and Savior. If we do, we will be saved from eternal death in Hell to eternal life in Heaven.

Final Stop on the Roman Road to Salvation...

Results of Salvation

Romans 8:1: *"Therefore, there is now no condemnation for those who are in Christ Jesus."* By accepting Jesus' death as a payment for our sins, we will never be condemned for our sins.

Romans 5:1: *"Therefore, since we have been justified through faith, we have peace with God through our Lord Jesus Christ."* Peace with God means we have been reconciled to Him through Jesus Christ. We can now have a relationship with the living God because sin no longer separates us from Him.

Are you uncertain that if you were to die today you would go to Heaven? Have you followed the Roman Road to salvation? Will you accept Jesus Christ as your Lord and Savior today? You can **pray** to God right now and claim the promises of His word as your own.

- Admit that you have sinned against God and ask Him for forgiveness.

- Believe that the Lord Jesus Christ is the Son of God Who died for you on the cross, rose from the dead, and is Lord.

- Call upon Jesus Christ to be your Lord and Savior.

If you have accepted Jesus as your Lord and Savior today, we praise God for your decision! We encourage you to grow in your walk with God by praying to Him, reading the Bible, and joining a Bible believing church. Share with others the Roman Road to salvation, so they too may know of God's love and amazing grace.

*new-testament-christian.com. © New Testament Christian

If you have any questions concerning what you've just read, contact me through my website – www.barbaraeubanks.com.

Blessings in Jesus,
Barbara Eubanks

*Amazon Hope is not only a boat, but it is also a mission organization headed up by Ty Harris. It gives many people each year the opportunity to go down the Amazon River to remote villages where they share the gospel and bring many souls to Christ. If you would like more information about this ministry, call Ty Harris at **1(256)-458-4427** or email amazonhopemissiontrip@gmail.com. Go to the web site - http://www.amazonhope.org/ to find other ways you can participate.

About the Author

Barbara Eubanks, widow of Reverend Steve Eubanks, mother of three sons, and grandmother to eight is a Christian humorist, speaker, and author. Her life has been unorthodox in that she married at age fifteen and had birthed her three sons by age twenty. When the children were young, she began to further her education and earned three degrees – B.A. from Samford University and M.A. and Ed.S from the University of Alabama.

After teaching high school English for thirty-five years, God led her to a new career. She has written three humorous devotional books and two novels: *Humorous Happenings in Holy Places* (2004), *And the Angels Laughed* (2006), *Laughing with the Lord* (2010), *A Web too Tight* (2012) and *A New Beginning: God's Second Chances* (2017). In addition, she has written numerous magazine articles. She entertains and inspires with Christian humor in her monthly "Holy Humor" column for *Anniston/Gadsden Christian Family Magazine* and previously was a regular writer for *Event Marshall County Magazine.* Eubanks has also developed and published Sunday school lessons for *LifeWay.*

She now resides near Albertville, Alabama, where she and her husband built their home on farmland homesteaded by her great-grandfather.

Contact Barbara Eubanks for speaking events: email - Barbara@barbaraeubanks.com

Website – www.Barbaraeubanks.com

www.ingramcontent.com/pod-product-compliance
Lightning Source LLC
Chambersburg PA
CBHW071328250626
47159CB00004B/1505